ABOUT THIS BOOK

Every town has stories of its past, and Havenwood Falls is no different. And when the town's residents include a variety of supernatural creatures, those historical tales often become Legends. This is but one . . .

Gregory and Charlotte left their lives as pirates behind to huddle in a tinker's shop, building fantastic creations powered by steam and aether. Fifteen hundred miles inland from the ocean they once called home, they only seek a quieter, safer way of life in the mountains of the Colorado territory. Fixing their neighbors' watches, creating beautiful and unique gifts, and helping to protect the burgeoning town is how they hope to make up for their past life of misdeeds.

Becoming a target of a crazed fae was not part of the plan.

The couple put their abilities and creations to the test to do everything they can to defend their new settlement. But their search for redemption from their wayward past may come to an end if death finds them—and their newfound family—first.

REDEMPTION'S END

A LEGENDS OF HAVENWOOD FALLS NOVELLA

ERIC R. ASHER

LEGENDS OF HAVENWOOD FALLS BOOKS

Lost in Time by Tish Thawer

Dawn of the Witch Hunters by Morgan Wylie

Redemption's End by Eric R. Asher

Trapped Within a Wish by Brynn Myers

Blood and Damnation by Belinda Boring (August 2018)

Fated Beginnings by E.J. Fechenda (September 2018)

More books releasing on a monthly basis

Also try the signature NA/Adult series, Havenwood Falls, and the YA series, Havenwood Falls High

Stay up to date at www.HavenwoodFalls.com

Sometimes there is magic in the steam.

CHAPTER 1

"How can you stand the noise in here?" Charlotte asked.

I kept my eyes on the seemingly random array of tiny gears and screws under the magnifying glass in front of me. Trying not to give myself away, I screwed the top back onto the flask in my left hand and slid it under the workbench.

"What noise?" I asked. I pulled another lens over my larger magnifier and carefully screwed one of the cogs back together. Only then did I turn away and look up at my wife, not missing the subtle frown and crease of her brow above her light brown eyes.

"No need to hide your flask," Charlotte said. "Even if I hadn't seen your clumsy ass trying to hide it, it smells like a still in here. I'm sure that's just what our customers want to see—you drunk, Gregory."

I sheepishly held out the bronze flask to Charlotte. "Just testing."

Somehow Charlotte managed to take a long swig out of the flask without breaking eye contact. The woman knew me too well, and I loved it.

"Who are you making that automata for?" Charlotte asked,

1

indicating the detached body, limbs, and tiny gears strewn about the workbench. When it was assembled, it would be an intricately animated dancer. Now it was, admittedly, a bit of a mess.

I took the flask back as she handed it to me, narrowing my eyes and taking a small sip. The slightly sweet moonshine burned its way down my throat before settling as a fire in my gut. "This one's just for the shop."

"Another bauble without a buyer," Charlotte muttered. "You need to finish those watches. At least until we find out there's a fence in town for some of our . . . less legitimate keepsakes, as I don't think the bank will accept stolen art. We can afford two more loan payments on the shop with what we have in cash. Maybe. We've barely been here a year, and the town has been here longer than that. I don't want to leave a bad impression on the banks."

I pinched the bridge of my nose and took a deep breath. "I know."

"Sure," Charlotte said. "What you really mean to say is that you find working on those pocket watches boring. And I understand that, I really do. But you aren't getting paid by the city again until you finish the conservatory. And that's if those contraptions will even work."

"They'll work," I said. "They have to. With all the creatures . . ."

"Species," Charlotte said, correcting me.

I nodded. "With all the species coming here, the town needs protection. Werewolves and vampires are peoples' neighbors in this place, but I don't think they fully understand the threat a fae can represent. Especially the Unseelie fae."

Charlotte settled into the workbench beside me. It used to be we could share the workbench, like one giant communal space. But if I was being honest with myself, I'd grown sloppy in my old age. There was a method to the chaos, and I always knew which screws went with which part and what springs I'd removed from which frame, but to the casual observer, it was pure chaos.

But beside me, Charlotte's workstation was pure order. She could chisel and carve wood, building the most intricate locks and puzzle boxes you can imagine, from the picture in her mind. There were a few things I could build from memory. I preferred to draw things out ahead of time. So in addition to three dozen jars of screws and fifty different trays of tiny parts, my workspace was littered with paper.

"You sell many more of those puzzle boxes," I said, "I won't need to worry about fixing those watches, or selling moonshine."

The front door—a thick heavy thing with a great deal of intricate carvings—swung open. Some of the patterns were subtle, but if someone had grown up around the tinkers' guilds, they were sure to recognize a few. And if they had grown up in the company of pirates, they were likely to recognize the vague outline of the crossbones formed from old iron.

Theodore, my apprentice, glanced back at the hinges as he crossed the threshold. He'd let his sandy brown hair grow to the point that he looked more like some of the soldiers I'd known in the east than the neatly groomed young man I was used to.

"You finally got the hinges to stop squeaking? They didn't even whisper."

The door snapped closed a moment later, and welcome chimes sounded. While I may have been able to fix the squeaking hinges, I was still having trouble regulating the volume of the chimes. They thundered to life, playing a quick four-note arpeggio that one might mistake for a thunderclap.

Theodore threw his hands over his ears, but by the time he managed to cover them, the chime was already done.

"Sorry about that," I said.

"What?" Theodore asked, slowly lowering his hands.

"I changed my mind," Charlotte said. "I think you should focus on fixing that damn chime."

"All in good time," I said, shooting her a crooked smile.

I stood up from the bench, carefully lifting the leather apron over my head. It held nearly as many tools as I had strewn across the workbench. "Ready for a little hike?"

"I'm ready to learn how to run those stills," Theodore said.

Charlotte slowly raised an eyebrow. "I believe what Theodore means is that he'd like to learn how to run the stills without blowing himself up."

I frowned slightly and nodded. "As I said."

I hung the apron on a small rack sunk into the wall. I pulled a discreet lever, capped with a polished walnut handle, and the entire rack sank into the wall, only to be replaced by a display of some of Charlotte's finest puzzle boxes.

"How cold is it today?" Charlotte asked.

"You haven't been out?" Theodore asked.

Charlotte shook her head. "Haven't needed to yet. Living above the shop is rather convenient like that."

"I'd say it's close to sixty."

"Take your coat," Charlotte said, eyeing me as I circled around the workbench very much without my coat.

"I don't think that's really necessary," I said.

"It doesn't matter if you think it's necessary," Charlotte said. "Take your coat."

I blinked at my wife, and while I pondered arguing for a moment, I instead hurried to the back, grabbed my coat, and joined Theodore in the front of the store. "We'll be back in a few hours."

"If you're not," Charlotte said, "I'll assume you're dead."

Theodore laughed, but he shut up when I shot him a cutting glare.

I rolled the cuff of my coat back and checked the watch sewn into the lining. It would likely take a half hour to hike to the stills if we didn't run into trouble. That would give us two hours before we needed to head back. "I'll take you out for a fine dinner tonight," I said.

Charlotte harrumphed. "As long as you're not cooking it, it should be fine indeed."

I leveled my gaze at her. "Charlotte."

She grinned at me and shooed us out the front door. I sighed when the chimes sounded again as the door closed behind us.

"Let's get on with it then," I said.

Most of the town had gravel streets now, but a few places tended to get muddy enough to trap a wagon wheel. I glanced back at the shop as my boots crunched in the rock. When we first opened the store, it had been my decision to simply put up a sign that said horologist. Charlotte protested, saying too many people wouldn't realize that we even sold watches, much less puzzle boxes and automata. As usual, she'd been right. So below the word horologist, we now had gilt lettering that said, "Timepieces, Music Boxes & Gifts."

I took a deep breath and smiled at the brick façade lined with rich lumber. It had long been our dream to leave our old seafaring life behind and open a shop, and it gave me hope that life would be good in this new town.

"You okay?" Theodore asked, pulling me out of my thoughts.

"I'm excellent, son," I said, pulling my coat a little tighter against a chilly breeze. "Into the woods."

CHAPTER 2

*T*he town had come a long way in the months since Charlotte and I moved in. Or had it been a year now? I tended to lose track of these things when I was focused on my work. It was easy to let the days slide by, exchanging one set of dangers for another. From the outside, frontier life looked softer than life on the seas, but they were both hard.

I helped design some of the buildings here. Others were a bit more what I would call clunky. Inefficient architecture and designs that served no real purpose other than a rural Main Street aesthetic I'd seen a dozen times before. I supposed that was well and good. Most people wouldn't want their town to look like a square box. What truly set the view apart were the mountains—soaring, majestic things that reminded me of the white-capped waves in a squall.

My gaze lingered on the conservatory we'd been repairing on the back of the inn. The structure was mostly a framework now, as we had to pull the glass down to get to the root of the problem, and I doubted anyone would realize what I'd hidden there. It had taken some convincing to get Mihail, the inn's owner, to let me include the ward designs, but that wasn't the kind of thing you did without permission. Or, at least not without partial permission. This was especially true when the owners were vampires. They may have understood the threat of other vampires, and even hunters, but I suspected they hadn't had dealings with the darkest side of the Unseelie fae like Charlotte and I had.

The rock and dirt of the streets gave way to trees and the meandering creek. Theodore and I followed the old creek north into the mountains. In the distance, I heard the faint crashing of the waterfalls.

There was something both reassuring and threatening about the more remote parts of the woods. It would take some time to reach the stills, as they were deeper into the wilderness, closer to the falls. I was pretty sure Theodore felt the same way about our isolation. I caught his gaze flickering from one side of the path to the other, trying to locate whatever wildlife was bouncing around the trees above us. It was early in the day, but not much sunlight reached the forest floor, leaving us in a surreal world of shadows.

WE HADN'T RUN anything through the stills in a couple weeks. Not only because I was behind on the projects and repairs in the shop, but because the heavy rains in the springtime tended to wash out the path around the creeks. And a small footbridge that only spanned half of the raging current of water wasn't much good to anyone. I wasn't too happy about the delay occurring right after we replaced the still Theodore had destroyed.

We spent most of the walk in silence, only the sounds of the forest keeping us company along with the crunch of underbrush beneath our boots. The kid may have been young enough to maintain a conversation during the more difficult parts of the hike, but I wasn't nearly so young as him. In some ways, I supposed I was jealous of his easy stride up the side of the mountain, but I'd never want to live through those years again. Charlotte and I were building a new life, in what I hoped was a safer place. We weren't exactly spoiled for choices.

I slowed as we crested the ridge, and a small spiral of steam curled up from the shack that stored our stills. In the year since I'd set up, no one had bothered the operation. I didn't really know if it was simply because our neighbors were all good people, or they understood the dangers of the still, or perhaps the smells were overwhelming to those with enhanced senses. In any case, the steam meant someone had been here, or was still here.

That wasn't to say I'd never seen anyone in the area before, and I was nothing if not cautious. I slid the sleek form of a small pistol out of a hidden pocket in my coat. From another pocket, I pulled the strange clip of ammunition and cylinders that gave the gun its name: the harmonica pistol. It wasn't until I slid the ammunition home and cocked the gun that Theodore realized what was in my hand.

"What are you doing?"

"Someone's here," I said. "And I'm getting ready to greet them."

"Oh," Theodore said. "It was me. I pulled the mash and fired up the stills yesterday. I just wanted you to see that I'm not an idiot."

I slowly raised an eyebrow. "I told you not to touch these things without me. That's not a complicated instruction, is it?"

"It's fine," Theodore said, biting off the words. "Yes, of course I understand. But I've been following you around up here for six months, and you haven't let me touch a damn thing."

I frowned at the anger in Theodore's words.

"No," I said, "and when you didn't listen? We lost a still."

The boy had always been patient, but perhaps he was reaching the end. He was recently in his twenties, and I had a fuzzy remembrance of being that age myself. I took a deep breath, trying to will my frustration away. But Theodore had managed to blow one of our stills up, and it could have been him, if he'd been standing too close. I didn't want to be the one to explain that to his parents, or any part of his family.

"What time did you start yesterday?" I asked.

"About noon," Theodore said, some of the anger bleeding out of his words. "I made sure to mark it."

I nodded and started toward the plain cedar door, considering the idea I should put a lock on the shack. I slid through the doorway, sweeping my pistol around the room before releasing a breath I hadn't realized I'd been holding.

"What do we have?" I asked as I hooked the pistol into a loop on my vest and checked the pressure on the still. Theodore had obviously put an adequate amount of fuel in, but not enough to cause a rupture. It was still good on water, which meant as long as he had a proper mixture of corn, sugar, yeast, and water, this batch of moonshine should be just fine. But something didn't smell quite right. It smelled too mature, too rich. I frowned.

"I did it just like you always told me to. The only thing different is the stream was a little muddy."

"You put muddy water in the still?" I asked, unable to hide the disgust in my voice.

"Of course not," Theodore said. "I went a little farther upstream. Where the pond is."

"The pond?" I asked. "You put water from the pond in here?"

I hadn't explained to him exactly why that was a bad idea. He didn't know what Charlotte and I knew. I bit my lip and thanked the stars that the stills hadn't blown up again. That didn't do much to alleviate the slightly more concerning thought that the stills could blow up in our face now.

"Shut the fires down," I said. "Whatever we have, we have. We need to shut this down now."

"I've done it before."

"Kill the fire now. We'll lose the whole still. Again."

Theodore didn't ask me to clarify. We went about our business, throwing the lever to cut off the airflow around the fires underneath the still. He pulled another lever to drop the tray of charcoal out from underneath and slid it into a fire pit in the corner of the shack.

I turned the nozzle on the collection barrel and whistled when a clear stream of moonshine splashed down into my copper mug, with one small side effect. A subtle golden light glowed from the normally crystal-clear liquid.

"What is that?" Theodore asked.

"There's something I have to tell you about that old waterfall, and the pond you took this water from."

I took a deep breath through my nose over the copper cup in my hand, surprised to find the usual burning aroma of fresh moonshine, but there was something else. The water Theodore had used had imbued it with something more. I pondered the mug for a moment, before deciding I'd lived a good life and took a sip.

I winced at the ungodly sear, but exhaled slowly as the burning left and a slightly sweet aftertaste remained. I ran my tongue across my teeth and sighed.

"That pond is where we harvest the aether. It's in the very waters. Whatever placed it there, of which I'm fairly sure was a magic beyond anything I've encountered before, also holds it there. It doesn't seem to be anywhere downstream. It stops at that pond."

Theodore blinked at me.

"But it's a pond," Theodore said.

I shrugged. "You've seen the power sources that fuel some of the automata. I've been filling vessels here for almost a year, and it hasn't diluted at all. Whatever it is, I think it might be more closely related to some of the strangeness around this town than any natural phenomena."

"Like someone put it there?"

I nodded. "There are a few beings I've heard of with the power to do it."

There was a time Theodore would've asked me more questions. Or he would have scoffed at my mention of supernatural things creeping along in the night. And something stalking the woods in broad daylight? Unthinkable. But we'd all seen things. Some of the families of the town had been open with Charlotte, and even a few with me. We knew there was a great deal more to our little town than one saw on the surface.

I took another sip, frowned, and looked down at my copper mug. Warmth flooded through me, sliding into my arms and down to my toes. That one sip felt more like a misguided night in my youth spent curled around a bottle of rum.

"I think this might be a little stronger than usual," I said. "Might even make the vampires happy."

Theodore frowned and stared at the stills for a moment, quite probably contemplating the still exploding. The kid had gotten lucky the first time. I was glad he hadn't blown himself up, or the new still.

"Old man, are you there?" a voice shouted from outside the shack.

I muttered under my breath, fairly certain the man would be able to hear every word. "Let me do the talking. I don't want you going and getting shot. Or worse."

CHAPTER 3

I raised my voice and said, "I'm here. And I have Theodore with me."

"You going to ask me in?"

"I thought that was just a legend," I said.

The voice on the other side of the door chuckled, and light flooded the shack as Roman, one of the Bishop brothers, stepped inside. Charlotte thought the man was handsome—debonair was the word she'd used. I knew his ilk. I suspected if he lived long enough, he'd have far less savory dealings than running moonshine. We'd have used him as bait on the galleons we once sailed.

"You're not so skeptical as most," Roman said, brushing dark hair away from his ocean-blue eyes. "But I already told you, I am no vampire."

"You hear stories," I said. "I suppose you heard our whole conversation?"

Roman hesitated, and I suspected he was pondering whether or not to play dumb in an effort to use the information as leverage at some later date. I rather thought he'd make a great politician someday, and I wasn't particularly fond of politicians. After a time, he nodded.

"Many of us in town already know about the pond. But I must admit, we hadn't thought about making moonshine out of it."

I barked out a harsh laugh. "That's because most of you have a better sense of self-preservation than my apprentice here."

Roman looked at Theodore and studied him for a moment. I took a deep breath, forcing myself to remain calm despite being in the presence of a creature I didn't fully understand. He wasn't entirely human, of that I had no doubt. Roman turned his attention back to me, his gaze boring into mine. "Have you thought about my offer? In all my years, I haven't met a bootlegger that could make a moonshine like yours."

"There are plenty of moonshiners out there that can do better than me." I held out the copper mug.

Roman frowned at it for a moment, and then apparently decided that he too had lived long enough. He sniffed at the rim of the mug before draining it in one long gulp. I studied Roman's face, watching his subtle frown lift slightly and the crease of his brow relax.

"Not bad?" I asked.

"You could sell this at every bar in town."

"We only have one bar."

"For now," Roman said. "I know you're not earning enough to keep that shop running. How many of the people who live here even know what horology is?"

I bristled at his words before muttering some rather inappropriate curses at Roman.

He smiled. "I was just trying to make a point."

Roman took a deep breath and settled onto a stool near the door. "Charlotte has been more open about your financial situation. She seems willing to entertain me handling distribution."

The liquor was clearly beginning to affect Roman, and that surprised me. He sighed and crossed his arms. He looked more relaxed than I'd seen him since I'd known him.

I crossed my arms, mimicking Roman's pose. I knew he'd spoken to Charlotte, and perhaps he thought he'd been subtle about it. That irritated me. But the simple fact of the matter was that we needed the deal, and I might be able to use it to get Roman's unwitting help.

I nodded. "I do have a condition. Two actually."

Roman inclined his head.

"Keep everyone away from the conservatory tomorrow. And if anything happens to me or Charlotte, you'll treat Theodore as you would me. With respect."

Roman's lips curled into a smile. "You're a brave man to demand what can be taken so easily."

"Make the deal," I said.

Bishop studied my hand for only a moment, then reached out and exchanged grips. "You'll be making some serious coin off of this, old man. You made the right choice."

"Be in the conservatory at daybreak," I said. "Make sure it's cleared out. I'll have a contract drawn up."

"Of course you will. See you around, Theodore." He paused at the doorway. "I understand there's an Unseelie fae that's taken some issue with you. Maybe they heard about your agreement to install the wards and didn't much like it." With that, Roman Bishop left.

I blinked at the empty doorway.

"You said yes," Theodore said.

"We need the money, and I imagine the Bishops will be more discreet than a lot of runners would be. I'm somewhat more concerned how Roman knew about the wards."

"The good news is he probably wants you alive," Theodore said. "You'll be his new supplier, after all."

I harrumphed. "We shall see."

I wondered if there was more to Bishop's warning, if something from our past had caught up to us.

Theodore pursed his lips, but said no more.

"Fill a few jars," I said. "We'll take them back to the shop. There's work to be done. We have to prep the wards for the conservatory, and we only have until sunrise to finish them."

The trek back may not have been any longer, but it was most assuredly more effort carrying a few large jugs of moonshine. Theodore had bound four of them together and stuffed them into a large sack. Almost every step he took, I worried that he was going to overbalance and tumble down the mountain. Or worse, break a jar.

Once we were back onto the relatively flat roads, the walk wasn't nearly as strenuous. My boots thudded on the wooden walkway outside the shop, and I pulled the door open to let Theodore in first. He shuffled past, careful not to smack the doorframe with the load he was carrying. The door had barely closed behind me when the thunderous chimes announced our arrival.

Charlotte grimaced and raised an eyebrow.

"I'll get to it," I muttered, glancing back at the calamity of chimes.

"Of course you will."

"Theodore knows about the aether," I said.

"Well, it's about time," Charlotte said. "He does have a key to the store, after all."

"He also ran the pond water through the still again," I said.

Charlotte's other eyebrow rose to join the first. "I confess I'm rather surprised to see both of you alive."

"The batch is surprisingly good," I said.

"You *drank* it?" Charlotte asked.

"It's not like it's the first time," I said. "We've been swimming in that pond before, before we realized what was."

"That wasn't distilled into a concentrated form," Charlotte said. "Lord above, that could have killed you both."

Theodore slowly untied the satchel after setting it on the workbench. His gaze flicked between me and Charlotte, and I suspected he was wondering if it was safe to speak.

"We're getting low on the vessels for aether," Charlotte said. "I checked the safe upstairs, and it looks like we only have a few left."

I grimaced before nodding. "The conservatory ward has to go up at daybreak. We should have enough vessels for the morning. Roman Bishop is going to draw everyone away from the conservatory. I'll have those defenses installed whether the innkeeper's agreed to it or not."

"What are the defenses?" Theodore asked.

"My great-grandmother used to call them wards," Charlotte said. "Protection against the Unseelie fae." She glanced at me. "I assume we're telling him everything at this point?"

I nodded. I didn't really see a point in keeping anything else from Theodore. If he was going to live as a human among the monsters, he needed to understand.

He needed to be ready.

CHAPTER 4

"Why is Roman Bishop going to help you with this?" Charlotte asked. "The Bishop boys have never seemed very fond of you."

I harrumphed.

"What have you gotten us into?"

"Nothing. I took Roman up on his offer to distribute our moonshine. That's it." I patted one of the jugs on the workbench. "And he's planning on selling this new aether brand at a premium. We may yet get out from under that banker."

Charlotte frowned, her lips just barely turning down at the edges. She was considering my words, and probably weighing the benefits of working with the Bishops against the weight of our debts. It was much the same argument I'd had in my own head.

"So be it." She nodded. "We need to do something."

"I know," I said quietly. "It's why I said yes."

Charlotte sighed.

"So what exactly are we doing tonight?" Theodore asked as he walked back into the room. He'd left for a short while after I'd told him it had been his girlfriend, Betsy, who had designed the wards. "And what do we need to do at the conservatory in the morning?"

A slow smile spread across my lips.

I exchanged a glance with Charlotte. Something that I'd truly come to enjoy about being in a relationship as long as we had been was that much communication could occur in just that glance. I couldn't really explain it, whether it was the tilt of the eyes, or the body position of the other person, but it was like we could carry on entire conversations without speaking a word.

I wanted to be sure she agreed with telling Theodore everything, and when she blinked once, slowly, I knew she did.

I turned my attention back to Theodore. "This place is a haven for people, and creatures, that are different from much of the world. And while most of the folks here may be the peaceful sort, we all have histories."

"What do you mean by histories?" Theodore asked. "I mean, we've all known some bad people . . ."

"These aren't just bad people," Charlotte said. "Settlers are going missing."

Theodore frowned slightly. He'd heard the rumors, stories of some of the stranger creatures that had been sighted around the town. People still liked to share stories around the campfire, even when those tales had more truth in them than the listeners may have known.

"There are Unseelie fae nearby." I let the words hang in the air, waiting for Theodore's reaction.

Theodore frowned. "What can we do?"

"Fae can die if exposed to iron," I said.

"Is that what we're doing at the conservatory?" Theodore asked. "Ironwork?"

I shook my head. Charlotte held up one of the aether vessels. "You've seen these before."

Theodore nodded.

"Gregory has designed them to work as a power source. And they can power a great many things."

"Combined with iron and wards, it makes for an effective defense against the Unseelie fae. That's what we're setting up in the conservatory. I think we can shield the entire town with three strategically placed wards. The inn, the saloon, and the meeting hall."

Charlotte glanced at me and frowned. "But we have concerns. The wards are fae wards, and if the fae themselves can be poisoned by iron, I worry what might happen. Will the iron cancel out their magic, or render it too weak to be useful? We'll test it tomorrow."

I studied Theodore for a short time. "We won't know until we try. It's better than anything we have right now. Charlotte can provide an amulet to the innkeeper that will offer protection to even an Unseelie fae should they choose."

Charlotte nodded. "You might want to call Betsy over for dinner. We have a lot of work to do tonight."

BETSY WAS one of those strange people who loved to cook. She had her hair pulled up into a braid that didn't look so different from Charlotte's, other than its jet black color. I'd suspected Betsy was something more than human the first time I'd met her, as even Charlotte had commented on her ethereal beauty. But it was also the only reason I could come up with as to why in the world she would be running around with Theodore, a brash young man most would consider far less attractive than Betsy.

"Disgusting," Charlotte said, eyeing the giggling couple as they worked on installing a handful of our smallest vessels.

"We used to be like that," I said.

Charlotte harrumphed. "Maybe in your head," she muttered. "Maybe."

I scraped up the last bittersweet bread from my plate before picking up everyone else's dishes and taking them to the wash bucket in the back. It was more of a trough, I supposed, just a bit cleaner than what you'd let the horses drink out of. I let the small stack of dishes clink to the bottom where, if I was being honest, they'd probably soak for several hours.

My boots thudded on the hardwood floors as I made my way back to the workbench and settled in beside Charlotte. She was putting the finishing touches on one of her intricate gift boxes, more or less a bribe for the Petrans, the owners of the inn, for letting us work in the conservatory. For a moment, I didn't focus on my work; I just watched Charlotte. She moved with the deft motions of someone who had practiced their art for a very long time. There was no uncertainty as she slid fragile bits of wood into a baffling alignment that would only open when someone inserted one of the aether pendants, or broke the box open entirely. She fiddled with the lid and tightened the ratio on the wooden gears used to withdraw the locking bars.

"Pass me that pendant, would you," Charlotte said, "if you're just going to stare?"

I smiled and slid the slightly luminescent pendant closer to her. Her fingertips brushing mine, she took the locket and placed it on top of the puzzle box. The faint glow of the trapped aether etched its way across the box until the polished crystal she'd inlaid in the wood burst into life, and the mechanism inside clicked. The faintest echo of wood sliding across wood preceded the lid of the box slowly creeping open. Charlotte smiled at her handiwork, and I shook my head.

"That's a fine gift," I said. "Are you sure you want to give it away? I don't know if we have the finer?"

"There will always be more boxes. I think more might sell with the aether pendants. It's attractive."

"I'd certainly buy one," Betsy said. "My mother loved puzzle boxes."

"We can take a small one," Theodore said. "Leave it on her grave?"

Betsy gave him a smile and patted his shoulder.

I pulled the spring-loaded lever off the shelf behind the workbench. It had a long empty space in the middle, almost like a lathe that I would use to turn wood, but this was something quite different. Once the lever was securely mounted to the workbench, I pulled one of the folded iron plates out from the hidden drawer beneath the workbench. Some tinkers I'd known would go so far as to create hidden panels all across their shop, but I generally found that hiding something under the table was good enough.

The plate itself was mounted to a cylinder, and when its twelve sections were folded together, it looked like little more than the head of a walking cane. An unbalanced and perhaps ugly cane, but a cane nonetheless.

I pulled the lever, which struck the mechanism at the center of the pole, causing the plate to fan out and the small receptacle to become exposed. I slid one of the aether vessels into the pipe, not so unlike loading a bullet into a rifle. Once it was seated, I released the lever and let the plate slap closed once more.

"Are you bringing that one?" Theodore asked. "It looks like the ones you use in the automata, just bigger."

I shook my head. "It's similar, but it's not the same. This one will fit into the pipes that run along the conservatory. You remember the broken pipe you pointed out last week?"

Theodore nodded.

I pulled the cylinder off the lever and held it up. "This will fill that gap, and the aether will flow through the ward etched into this plate."

"You really think that gadget will power a ward?" Betsy asked.

I nodded.

"Where in the world did you get a fae ward?" Betsy asked. "Those aren't exactly common knowledge. Although, not so uncommon around here, I suppose."

I blinked at her. She'd given it to us. Was this a less-than-subtle way of telling us not to tell Theodore? I glanced between the two.

"Yes, I know she gave you the ward," Theodore said, exasperated. He turned to Betsy. "Is this really the time for more mischief?"

She grinned at him.

"It's not active when it's collapsed," I said, returning my attention to the ward. "Only when we install it will it activate."

"These aren't weapons," Charlotte said. She eyed Theodore for a moment. "They won't defend you from what's out there. You've seen them. Around the still, near the old mine."

Theodore nodded. "The man of shadows."

"So dramatic," Betsy said.

CHAPTER 5

*I*t took more effort to keep our work clean as the night wore on. We needed precision in the assembly to allow the wards to work. When Theodore's head started to fall forward and his grip became loose on the ward he was working on, Betsy snatched the ironwork away.

My gaze may have been a bit too sharp, as she gave me an odd look.

Betsy glanced at Theodore, and then back to me. "Did you expect it to burn me?"

I blinked at the question.

"You've been good to Theodore," Charlotte said. "You've been good to us. There is no quarrel here, only the insatiable curiosity of a tinker."

I narrowed my eyes. "I can tell she's keeping secrets."

Betsy grinned. She glanced at Theodore, who was now half bent over on the workbench and snoring. "I like this town, and I like the people that have come here. I want no harm done to them."

I ran my finger across the rune etched in one of the plates that formed the ward. "You must like us if you've offered your family's magic."

Betsy didn't respond. She only offered a small smile, then elbowed Theodore to wake him up. He woke with a start, almost falling sideways off his chair before Betsy caught him.

"What did I miss?" Theodore asked before releasing a wide yawn.

"Wordplay and shenanigans," Charlotte said. "The usual nonsense."

"Are you still playing this game, Gregory?" Theodore asked, eyeing me.

The question rankled. "It's not a game, boy. It's simply a concern for Betsy's well-being, and ours. Fae magicks can be quite dangerous, to both the user and the target."

"You could be a politician with words so smooth as that," Betsy said.

"No, he couldn't," Charlotte said.

I snapped the last pole out of the levering mechanism and studied the panel on the back. Theodore had done the metalwork on parts of this one. The grooves fit together perfectly, so no man, or creature, could fit so much as a hair into the grooves to pry open the aether chamber.

"It's good work," I said. "Damn good work."

"I think were done," Charlotte said. "Let's get packed up and ready to go."

"How many do we need for the morning?" Theodore asked. He gestured at the array of five plates and columns.

"We're only installing one," Charlotte said. "But take them all, in case we have issues when we try to install it."

"All of them?" Betsy asked. "Doesn't that seem a little excessive?"

"No," I said. "Charlotte's right. We haven't tested this on a structure as large as the inn and the conservatory."

Betsy nodded, apparently agreeing with the thought to some degree.

I looked at the clock on the wall, a mass of exposed gears and springs. We had about two hours before daylight. "If you want to, you're welcome to rest here. Or we can rendezvous in the morning."

"There's plenty of room in the guest room upstairs," Charlotte said.

"Let's just stay here," Theodore said. Betsy wrapped her arm around his and nodded.

"Until the morning then," I said.

"You're being too hard on that girl," Charlotte said, her voice barely above a whisper. "She has done nothing to us. She has done nothing to our friends. If she was a threat, we would've seen some semblance of it by now. No creature is so patient as to sit among their prey for a year."

"But—"

"No," Charlotte said. "You approach everything as if it's a threat. And sometimes you're right. But you've also alienated some of our greatest friends, and befriended some of our greatest enemies. And I think it's made you paranoid, Gregory. Theodore is a smart boy. I'm telling you, we should trust her until we see different."

"She touched the iron tonight," I said.

"Yes," Charlotte said. "She's clearly not an Unseelie fae sent to infiltrate our clock shop."

I harrumphed, but the sheer level of sarcasm in Charlotte's words made me cringe.

"I'm not saying you need to apologize," Charlotte said. "All I'm saying is you could be a little more subtle in your suspicions. Not everyone is out to get you. No matter how much you deserve it," she added with a small laugh.

I grumbled and pressed a small button on the side of my end table. A mechanism inside started to turn, and the old woven cable that led up to the suspended lanterns above us slowly closed and snuffed the light with an old iron half sphere.

"That sounds a little squeaky," Charlotte said. She elbowed me in the ribs.

"Woman. You'll be the death of me." I rolled closer and snaked my hand across her waist. She settled in next to me, and I kissed her, lightly at first, until she responded.

A moment later, she pulled away and cracked one eye open. "Don't even think about it. Two hours of sleep is barely enough as it is."

"We're too old for this," I said with a small laugh.

Our short sleep came and went far too quickly. It felt as though I had barely closed my eyes, barely drifted off, before the gentle buzz on my nightstand grew into the dull calamitous roar of my bell alarm clock. It didn't take much to get dressed, as we hadn't really bothered to get into night clothes. Changing into something soft and warm sounded much more appealing at that moment than trudging our way across the square to the conservatory.

"Get a move on, then," Charlotte said. "You can put some coffee in that contraption of yours."

I nodded and started down the stairs with heavy, sleepy footsteps, surprised when I reached the bottom and found Theodore and Betsy waiting for us at the workbench. They almost looked chipper, which I found unusually irritating.

Theodore slid a mug of coffee toward me, and Betsy clinked the copper vacuum flask down beside it. "No time for breakfast. Let's go."

"There's always time for breakfast," Charlotte said. She pulled the basket off the counter behind her workbench and held out a scone she'd made the day before. You could almost say there was an art to eating leftover scones. They tended to turn into rocks, but if you soaked it in coffee or tea for just a moment, it made for a quick and easy snack.

I frowned at the small sea of crumbs the scone left in my mug before dumping everything into the copper vacuum flask. Charlotte took a few sips of coffee and added hers to the thermos as well. I figured that would be enough to get us through the morning.

"Let's find out if these Bishop brothers are worth their word," I said.

"If they hear you say that," Betsy said, "it's not their word you'll have to worry about."

"I've dealt with sharper blades in my day," I said.

"Your day was quite a while ago," Theodore said. "Charlotte might have to abandon you to the old folks soon."

Charlotte choked out a laugh. I gave her an exasperated look.

Betsy hefted one of the leather sacks that held the wards and the mechanics. I grabbed the other. Charlotte was better and faster than me with any gun, her vision sharper even now than I think mine had ever been. I'd rather her hands be free to take care of any issues that might arise than to be tangled up hauling around more tools.

"Let's get this done."

CHAPTER 6

*C*rossing the square so early in the morning was almost as uneventful as I'd hoped. There were more people out than I'd expected, but maybe that was part of Roman Bishop's plan. While I'd normally be focusing on some of the newer unfinished buildings going up, that morning found me glancing down every alleyway and checking every shadowed doorway. Would an old Unseelie fae be hiding behind one of those doors? I suspected they had never really come after us in earnest. And what rush did they have, really? Time wouldn't move the same for an immortal.

"We aren't alone out here," Betsy said, hurrying forward to step up beside me.

"I can see that," I said.

Betsy grimaced. "I can see more than you. I can feel more than you. And you know it. We're being followed."

My first instinct was to look over my shoulder, but my survival instinct told me not to do something so obvious. "Can you tell who?"

"No," she said. "I can only tell what."

"You're no fae," I said under my breath. This probably wasn't

28

the best time to grill Betsy about what she really was. But it might've been the best time to actually get an answer out of her, if she was worried about her own safety as well as ours. Or at least as well as Theodore's.

Betsy cursed under her breath. "I'm not."

"Of course you aren't," Charlotte said. "We've seen you handle iron like it was an inert piece of wood."

"We don't have time for this," Theodore hissed.

The total lack of curiosity in the boy's voice surprised me. I glanced back at him for a split second. "You already know." There was no accusation in my voice; it was simply a statement of fact.

"Of course he knows," Betsy said. "I'm a halfling. A halfbreed. Whatever horrible term you want to apply to me."

I blinked. I hadn't expected her to admit it so freely. A million things ran through my brain at once. With effort, I tamped down the rampaging questions in my head and asked the one that mattered. "What's behind us?"

"One fae, I think. It's hard to tell with all the iron we're carrying."

I took a deep breath and made a mental note that iron did affect Betsy, but it didn't seem to damage her physically.

The rest of the walk was far more tense. It felt longer, but nothing came from the shadows. No doorway creaked open as we passed, and nothing ambushed us from the alleys. We made our way past the most recently finished building closest to the end of the square, and as we turned the corner, the skeleton of the conservatory came into view. It was all copper and brass pipes with framing that housed a magnificent greenhouse. But now that we'd torn part of it down again, it was just dirt and metal and hope.

"Come," I said. "We may have a chance to test this far sooner than I would've preferred."

I made my way over to the pipes that would serve as the

irrigation lines. I absently noted that the wood for the flooring had been delivered far earlier than had been expected. That wasn't necessarily a great thing, as the weather might take its toll.

The satchel slid off my back, and I gently laid it next to the support in the middle of the conservatory. My gaze lingered on a patch of dirt that had clearly been dug up and repacked, but it was out of the way, and not my concern at that moment. To the untrained eye, the support may have looked like a simple metal beam propping up the bulk of the structure. But there was a small section about five feet off the ground that had what appeared to be a solid iron band wrapped around it. I held up one of the aether vessels to a small indentation in the plate, and the mechanism behind it clanked. The plate fell, revealing the recess that would hold the wards we'd mounted.

"It looks like Bishop kept his word," Charlotte said. "I don't see anyone."

I nodded. I could hear the surprise in Charlotte's voice, and it very much echoed my own. Roman struck me as someone who might keep his word to the letter of the law, but he also might twist the spirit of it like a fae.

I placed the pipe into the recess, and a small knob set inside rocked perfectly into the indentation on the bottom of the pipe. I twisted it so the ward plate would be facing out. Once it was balancing on its own, I reached back for the tool bag, realizing I'd left it too far away. "Theodore, palm wrench."

Theodore rooted through my pack for a moment, and then handed me a device that didn't look much like a wrench at all. It was flat and slender, and slid easily into the recesses of the opening in the beam. It took me a moment fishing around in the darkness, but eventually I felt the metal slide over the valve that would let me adjust the mechanism inside.

Two turns lowered a piston from above and secured the pipe on top and bottom. I pulled the palm wrench out and handed it back to Theodore.

"It didn't open," Betsy said.

"Not yet," I said, pulling the larger aether vessel out of my pocket. This one wasn't massive, and it wasn't camouflaged to hide the glow. I reached inside the pole and snapped it into the receptacle that I'd mounted and sited a month before. It burst to life, and for a split second, I could see the aether tracing the wires that led to the ward's mount.

I snatched my hand back, knowing that had I left it in there, I had a real risk of losing it. Two seconds later, the plates snapped out, far faster than anything we'd seen in the workshop. The iron clanged together, forming a circle for the light tracing the ward and bursting into brilliant life before fading back to a dull glow.

"It works," Charlotte said.

"Is that confidence I hear in your voice?" I asked, grinning at Charlotte.

Theodore helped me raise the iron cuff until it sat in place, concealing the plate. I placed the aether key on an indentation higher up the band, and the locking mechanism clicked home.

We stood silently for a moment.

"And it doesn't bother you?" Theodore asked. "You're sure?"

"I told you it wouldn't," Betsy said. "I wouldn't lie to you, Theodore."

"What have you done?" a voice hissed from somewhere behind us.

CHAPTER 7

I turned, snapping my gaze to the area I thought the voice had come from. Behind us, a slender form waited. I'd only seen him this close once, with his sword nearly at my throat as I escaped into one of the old mines. It seemed to be one of the few places he wouldn't follow. The man of shadows.

"Driscoll," Betsy said, her voice verging on a growl.

At first I thought his eyes were locked on Betsy, but as he shifted, and the wind caught the tails of his finely tailored jacket, I realized he was staring at the ward.

"What have you done?" Driscoll asked. He pointed at Betsy. "You would give these unevolved monkeys fae magicks? I can sense it behind the iron. Behind the inferior power of the witches."

"But can you see my friends?" Betsy asked.

"I see you well enough, halfbreed," Driscoll snapped.

"That wasn't my question."

Driscoll froze, his eyes darting around the construction area. "I should strike you down for this."

A slow smile crawled its way across Betsy's face. In the end, the expression was more like she had bared her teeth at Driscoll, and the effect was terrifying.

"It's working," she said, turning her back on Driscoll.

"You can't see us?" Theodore asked her.

"A side effect I'd hoped the wards would give—a shield to anything that lives inside these walls."

"They're still here," Driscoll said. It wasn't a question.

I came to realize that Betsy had deliberately tipped him off to the fact we were still standing here. A power play? Something more? The girl perplexed me, and the loyalties of any immortal always concerned me.

Driscoll's sword sang as he unsheathed it, a narrow blade that looked as if it could be bent between two fingers. But I had little doubt about the deadliness of that edge, or the fae who wielded it.

"You're weak," Betsy said. "And this town will defend itself against your will. Abandon your vendetta, and leave these people in peace."

Driscoll's face curled into a snarl. "You go too far, halfbreed." He charged.

Charlotte raised her rifle as the Unseelie fae closed on us. Betsy produced two short blades not so unlike the razor-thin sword wielded by Driscoll. She played her role well. Well enough that it unnerved me. But this was what we wanted.

This was not what Driscoll expected. He barked out a primal scream as his sword slid through the air toward Betsy. It didn't get far. As soon as his hand hit the threshold, the finger he had extended at the tip of the blade snapped back in a terrible crack. Surprise lit Driscoll's face for a second before he crashed into the invisible wall created by the wards. The faerie stumbled, catching himself in an obscenely graceful dip. He frowned and looked back up at Betsy. "You're a fool if you think that will keep me out."

"Then come in," Betsy said. "If you can."

An unnatural calm settled over Driscoll's face. "I will tear this house down, girl. And these people will know it was you that brought their end."

Clouds shifted above us, and as the shadows moved across the world, the shadowed man went with them.

"Did that go well?" Theodore asked. "Was that really bad?"

"Bit of both," Charlotte muttered.

"He issued you a challenge," I said, turning to Betsy.

She nodded and looked to the sky. "He'll return at the same time tomorrow. And he will keep his word."

I cursed. "How likely do you think it is he'll attack us before then?"

"Driscoll is known to be deceitful," Betsy said. "It is certainly a possibility."

"Then we stay together," I said. "You two come back to the shop with us. You can help me finish the wards before we all die horribly."

"Who could resist an invitation like that?" Charlotte asked. "I'll even serve you some stale bread for your last meal."

Betsy gave us a small smile as she slid her daggers back into her sleeves. Theodore just gave us a nervous laugh.

I pulled one of the portable wards out from the inside of my leather jacket and turned it over in my hand. "I would have liked to have tried this."

"I'm afraid you'll have your chance," Betsy said. "But I'm not sure you really want it."

We were walking away when I heard the first of the voices behind us, people returning to the inn from whatever distraction Bishop had set up. The construction workers would be back at their tasks without realizing what had happened, or what had been added to the conservatory.

I let out a relieved sigh as we crossed the threshold into our shop. It had been a long time since I'd fought any sort of battle. I didn't like the idea of going head-to-head with an Unseelie fae. If it had to happen, I was glad Charlotte was with me, and Theodore, and most especially Betsy.

"Thank you, Betsy," I said. "The ward clearly works."

She inclined her head.

"I thought Driscoll would use magic," I said. I had a sneaking suspicion he could cut us down without much effort.

"Most of the bloodthirsty fae I've known prefer to cut you open with their swords if they can," Betsy said. "Make no mistake—we insulted him, and it's going to get ugly."

I felt the reassuring weight of the clip for my harmonica pistol in my left breast pocket. It wasn't as portable as a revolver, and some would say it was not as reliable, but I'd come to know it quite well, and the ammunition was easy to manufacture.

"Even if the bullets fail," Betsy said, "the shields won't."

It was unnerving the way some people, and especially the fae, could read a human so easily.

"You and Theodore can make more money selling arms to the city," Charlotte said. "You wouldn't have to worry about what my crotchety old husband needs you for."

"Crotchety?" Theodore asked. "Is that a new term for cheap? Penny-pinching?"

"It's a new term for unemployed," I said slowly.

Betsy grinned at me and turned her attention to Charlotte. "I know we could. I know that would be a nice life for Theodore. But I have no desire for war."

"War?" I said.

Betsy remained quiet. And again I found myself wondering just how long she'd lived. How much she'd seen. And what she didn't tell us.

"When I was young, and lived in another place, there were wars. The humans rejected the half fae, and the Unseelie made to wipe us out. Not drive us from our home. They sought genocide. And it is why I help you now."

I often thought of war as the realm of man. As though humans were the only ones stupid enough to encourage the wholesale slaughter of their own people. But the more knowledge I'd gained of other beings, faeries and werewolves and things I once thought nothing but tales for children, I was coming to realize we were not unique for killing in this world.

"I will make you a thousand shields," Betsy said. "But I will not make your weapons. I will not give you a blade to pierce the heart of another, or a bullet to steal the life of a stranger.

"The journeys in past lives of the people who come to this settlement brought much darkness with them. There are darker things here. And there are darker things coming."

CHAPTER 8

"We need to get back to the mine," I said, rooting through the cabinet drawer that was now depleted of its usual load of ore. "I don't think I have enough to make the vessel for the meeting hall. It's not going to be enough to shield the town."

"Are you mad?" Betsy asked. "Driscoll's going to be watching for you. You think he won't be watching the mines?"

"We have to take that chance," I said. "He might be watching the stills."

"And if you're wrong?" Charlotte asked. "You think you'll dissuade him with what's in your pocket? You don't even know if that will work."

"What?" Betsy asked.

"Gregory carries the clip you etched for his gun."

"I am well aware of what I placed on it," Betsy said. "That old ward will prevent the metal from rupturing when he fires. What he chooses to do with what comes out of that barrel is of no consequence to me."

"Even if it changes the bullet?" Charlotte asked.

Betsy nodded.

The front door creaked open, and the clock chimes boomed into life a moment later.

"Are you open?" A slender man asked as he stepped inside. "I've heard you sell very fine puzzle boxes, and strange figures that can move on their own."

Charlotte's irritation flipped over to her smiling salesman persona in a second. "Automata, yes, of course we do. Is it a special occasion? A gift for a lady you're courting? I'm Charlotte, by the way."

"Lawrence," the man said, ignoring her other questions, instead staring at the wall of puzzle boxes and various watches we'd made and occasionally plundered over the years. "Lawrence Mills."

"Mills," I said. "You're one of the founders."

He nodded and gave me a small smile. "I heard you were taking action."

"Heard from who?"

"Mihail, at the inn. A few of us know of your past with the Unseelie. Some might wonder if you are . . . more worried than you need to be."

"Probably where Roman heard it then," I said under my breath, letting Lawrence's words slide off my back. I raised my voice a bit. "Best to be prepared."

Lawrence eyed Betsy for a moment, looked like he was going to say more, but remained silent. He stepped closer to one of the displays on the far side of the room.

"The automata are mostly in the cases," I said, inclining my head toward the wall of tall glass cabinets. "I'm not sure what your budget runs, but they're more expensive than most puzzle boxes."

"Gregory," Charlotte snapped. "That was rather rude."

I blinked. Some of the social niceties escaped me in my old age.

Lawrence held his hand out in a placating gesture. "It's fine," he said with a laugh. "No insult was taken."

"You see," I said. "Perfectly reasonable young man."

Charlotte turned slightly and scowled at me so Lawrence wouldn't be able to see.

"Are you shopping for a lover?" Betsy asked.

"Yes, and no. I'd like something that our grandchildren's grandchildren will still be able to enjoy long after we're gone."

Charlotte smiled and turned to the wall of puzzle boxes, pulling down a gold rectangular box. It was one of my favorites, with the mechanisms partially exposed, but hidden in intricate geometric patterns that surrounded a circle set in the middle.

"Oh, Christine would love that," Lawrence said, taking the box from Charlotte.

Charlotte held out a pendant. "This is the key. Placing it on top will start the lock opening."

Betsy turned to Charlotte. "Why don't you let Theodore and me take care of the shop? That delivery isn't going to wait."

Lawrence didn't seem to find anything strange about this conversation. And I rather admired Betsy's penchant for subtlety.

Charlotte nodded. "Of course. That's a wonderful idea. Come, dear."

We made our way into the back of the shop. Charlotte went straight for the armoire that was far more than it seemed. She opened the front of the massive piece, and at first glance, it appeared to hold nothing but sweaters and neatly folded trousers. When she pulled a hidden leather lever beneath the third shelf, a second layer opened, one that was partially sunken in the wall. Here were some of my stranger inventions: mechanical armor, swords that could be folded into their own selves, and ammunition that I'd not yet gained the confidence to test.

Charlotte pulled a pair of vambraces off one peg. She handed me the thicker one, and wrapped the other around her forearm. The front of the leather had what appeared to be random gears stuck to it, with a large gap in the center. But they weren't random—everything had a purpose. I handed her one of the cartridges from the inside of the right hand door, which she snapped into the opening on her vambrace. I did the same with mine, enjoying the satisfying click when everything locked together. I designed them for utility, and there were several different attachments we could use with the armor. The choice of shields seemed prudent for the day, but I also took the time to hand Charlotte a dark gray metallic cartridge. It was expandable, and held small bolts almost like a crossbow. In one accessory, we now had something to defend ourselves, and attack if needed.

Once we'd gathered up all we planned to take, I hefted the pack onto my back. It was unlikely anyone would steal the rudimentary mining equipment we'd left in the old caves, but I didn't want to hike all the way up there only to find we had nothing to help extract the ore.

I heard Theodore complimenting our patron's choice of puzzle box as we made our way out the back door. I exchanged a smile with Charlotte.

"He has some sense about him," Charlotte said as the door snapped closed behind us. "That will be useful to you."

"He's already quite useful," I said.

"I mean more useful than ruining your batches of moonshine, and trying to blow himself up."

"Fair point."

We made our way across town and followed the stream for a while. I waited until the sounds of the hammers, crashing boards, and what bustle there was in the town turned to nothing but a whisper.

"You're right," I said.

"About Betsy?" Charlotte asked.

I nodded.

"Of course I was." Charlotte lowered her voice. "What else could she be?"

"You mean your family didn't pass down ancient fae wards from generation to generation? I thought that was a regular dinner conversation for most families."

Charlotte blew out an exasperated breath. "At least you can admit when you're wrong. Watching Theodore twist his words up and ignore logic altogether, just so he doesn't have to admit he was wrong, is truly a spectacle."

"I know," I said. "But he means well."

We followed one of the rough mountain trails close to where the stills were at. Or at least close to where the path to the stills branched off. This time we continued on, climbing higher, making our way toward the Great Falls.

The sound of the falls crept up on us. You could hear them all the way from the town if you listened close enough and the birds were quiet enough, but it was different in the woods. It was always there, a little rush, the echoes of the stream winding through ancient rock. But the sound grew as we rounded a boulder, and the mountain split open before us.

Water crashed down into the pool at our feet, sending a fine mist into the air. It was a place you didn't want to be in the chilly months. My eyes trailed up the slope, half taking in the beauty, and half looking for Driscoll.

CHAPTER 9

"*L*et's get down there, then," Charlotte said.

I led the way off what to the naked eye looked like a ledge, but below the rounded face of a rock was a fractured stone that worked very much like an ill-formed staircase. When I first heard about the cave, or more like when I first stumbled onto it, I hadn't realized just how valuable it was. Some folks would be taken with the fancy gemstones and a few veins of precious metals found deeper in the cave system, but that's not why I was here. I was here for the strange ore. I'd tried crafting the aether vessels from gold and silver, copper and bronze, but they all failed. Some alloys lasted longer than others, but most couldn't survive the heat.

Aether itself didn't give off much heat, if any, but when used in devices like we concocted for the wards, it did. It wasn't what I thought of as natural heat, but one able to melt metal as it was while leaving flesh and wood untouched. I found it peculiar enough that I tried building a vessel out of wood, but the aether would seep through and eventually escape no matter how much I polished and sealed the outer layers. Only the ore in these caves mixed with iron seemed able to hold it. I only wished I knew what it was.

Down in the pool at the base of the falls waited boulders the size of horses. They sat in a pattern, spiraling out from the center of the falls. It was an ill-defined pattern, and I supposed many folks might not even consider it a pattern at all, but I'd spent enough time in the woods and streams to know that it wasn't natural.

"Something's above us," Charlotte said. She followed these words up with a small laugh, and her nonchalant approach sent a bolt of adrenaline down my back. It was a simple way to throw your enemy off, to not let on you knew they were there.

"Get in the cave," I said.

"I plan to," Charlotte said. "Of course, I have an old fool in front of me slowing me down."

I gave her a tight smile. We raised our voices, shouting to each other with the intent of seeming oblivious to whoever was watching. But we weren't oblivious. I'd seen the shadow now, near the top of the waterfall.

I waited until we rounded the back of one of the large boulders, which hid us from the eyes above. And I hissed, "Run!"

Sprinting across wet stone was a good way to break your body, but here it was even riskier. You get your foot caught in the wrong place, and the rivers swell, the waters would swallow you whole. Of course, the more obvious threat today was a bit more immediate.

Our boots splashed in puddles and echoed around the sunken pool. We'd almost reached the edge of the waterfall when I saw the shadow move above us. It was either a madman flinging himself to his death, or a faerie gifted with flight.

"Dive!" Charlotte shouted.

Next thing I knew, she'd pushed me forward. As I tumbled into the shadowed cave entrance, I saw the sword flicker through the waters above my head. Charlotte pulled the lever on the side of her vambrace, and a shield exploded out from the sides. She used it to batter away the sword before diving over me. Charlotte grabbed my wrist and yanked me toward the shadowy cavern. It was a small opening, but I'd sunken enough iron into the entrance to deter most fae. Nothing tried to follow us past the waterfall. The falls parted, and a snarling face appeared with water running down its ears and nose. Driscoll eyed the entrance to the cave, then flung himself back through the waterfall.

"He really doesn't like us much," Charlotte said.

I barked out a laugh. "Come on."

THE LANTERNS I'd left inside the cave several months before waited on a rickety wooden table. I remembered bringing Theodore here once and how he worried the lanterns wouldn't light with so much moisture in the air. That was before I showed him the fuel wrapped in the oiled leather pouches. I dropped two jagged white chunks into the lantern base and added a little water. We waited a few seconds before striking flint across the face of the lantern. The gas caught fire. The reflectors hooked on the little lanterns focused the light and pierced the shadows. Charlotte slid the mount of a lantern into her vest, and we made our way into the narrow section of the cave.

If I'd been much larger, the cave would've been impassable. As it was, the lantern on my own vest scraped against one wall while my shoulder blades scraped against the other. The passage was wider near the floor. I supposed I could've gone through on my stomach, but the cave had a tendency to take on water. And that seemed like a stupid way to die.

"I think I need to feed you less bread," Charlotte said. "Or we'll have to come up here and pry you out of this cave one day."

I didn't argue. She was right.

We only spent a few minutes in the narrows before the cave mercifully opened wide. It wasn't long before we could walk shoulder to shoulder without bumping into each other or the side of the cave. The glow of the lantern light glinted on some dusty metal in the distance.

"Looks like the equipment is still here," I said.

"Really, Gregory, who is going to climb into this mess and figure out how to drag that equipment out of here?"

"There are other passages through here. You never know if someone will find an easier way. We've dug a fairly deep channel into this mountain now." I shined my light at the timbers supporting the entrance to the tunnel I'd carved out over the past year.

The tunnel sloped downward and our conversation trailed off. Keeping our footing required more effort than at the relatively flat entrance to the cave. Theodore and I had carved wide rough steps into the steeper parts of the slope while leaving a smooth, almost ramp-like expanse to our right. It was down that ramp we let the heavier tools slide.

"Why don't you just leave all these at the bottom of the ramp?" Charlotte asked.

"Because if there's a cave-in, we'll lose all of our tools. It would be bad enough to lose the effort of digging this place out. Losing all our gear as well would take much longer to replace."

It wasn't long to the bottom of the curved tunnel, but it always felt significantly longer than it was. It was more damp than the mine above us had been. Part of it was cool and dry further in, until we finally reached the wall we'd been mining ore from.

While we didn't leave much equipment in the mine, we did leave the boilers at the bottom of the shaft. When they were filled with water, they were far too heavy to move. There was just enough of a trickle running down the ceiling that I was able to set up a sluice to refill them while we were out. Now one of them was overflowing, and I was glad I'd added an overflow release to keep the fuel below dry.

Charlotte lit the fire under the boilers while I studied the ore lodged in the wall. "I think we can stay on this vein that Theodore and I started." I ran my finger along a reflective gray streak embedded in the wall.

"You've gone deeper than I thought you would," Charlotte said. She pointed at the wooden support beams above me. "You're really stretching this out. You're going to need to get more lumber down here, and I don't think we can afford to hire anyone right now."

"Quite sure we can convince Betsy's friend to help us again. I never saw the man last time, and I suspect there's a very good reason for that."

"Fae?"

"That would be my suspicion."

Charlotte nodded. "It makes sense. Who else could have gotten timber in without being seen? Or at least without piquing someone's curiosity or leaving an obvious trail through the woods?"

I took a deep breath and turned back toward Charlotte. "The boilers ready?"

"Almost. The smaller one. Larger won't be ready for some time."

A few minutes later, the first hiss of steam punched through the release valve of the smaller boiler. I slid one end of the braided hose over the nearest valve and ratcheted a clamp down to hold it in place. Charlotte picked up the bigger end. She took what looked like deformed pickax heads out of the bag we'd dragged down and started attaching them to a belt that ran around the digger. Another minute and we were ready to start.

The fires turned the room into something more like a hot

spring. What had been relatively dry had now been saturated by the steam emanating from the boilers.

"Ready?" I asked.

Charlotte pulled a pair of goggles down over her face and rolled out the leather mask hanging beneath them. It would keep the worst of the debris away from her face, and protect her lungs all at once. She nodded.

I opened the valve on the boiler, and the hose spasmed. The braid expanded and fattened as the superheated steam rushed down. A cloud of white spewed from the side when Charlotte threw the lever.

The handheld digger roared to life, and Charlotte leaned into it, placing it against the wall where I'd indicated the vein of the gray ore.

What had been a quiet cave with nothing more than the hiss of fires became a deafening cacophony of machinery, broken stone, and crumbling ore. I grinned as I watched Charlotte work. She wielded the digger with more familiarity and ease than Theodore ever could. When the larger chunks of ore fell from the wall, I checked the clumps closer to me so I could scoop them up and drop them into a wheeled cart.

We stayed at it for another fifteen or twenty minutes before the digger clanged against something hard enough and deep enough to stop the sleeve of spinning pickax blades.

"Whoa!" I shouted.

Charlotte shut the valve, and the digger wound to a stop, the steam spraying from the side of the machine. I closed the valve on the boiler.

"What was that?" Charlotte asked.

"Looks like a large deposit of ore," I said, leaning in closer and adjusting my lamp so I could see the dented metal in the light.

"I don't think we're getting that out with the digger."

"I don't know if we're ever getting that out," I said. "And certainly not today."

Charlotte looked down at the ore loaded up in the small wheeled cart. "You think it's enough?"

I nodded. "Let's get back to the shop."

"Let's see if that wagon will float first," Charlotte said.

"I'm a little worried about that," I said with a nod. "This is a lot more ore, but I can't tell exactly how much metal is in each rock." I cursed. "I should've just built the pulverizer up here like I'd planned to."

"Of course. That would've been so subtle. I'm sure no one would've noticed you hauling all that equipment through the woods."

"Yes . . . Well . . ."

"We can load some of it into the packs. Just to be safe," Charlotte said.

"There's too much equipment in the packs," I said.

"Well," Charlotte said, "let's leave some of it here. At the bottom of the mine. It's not likely to flood this week, and no one's going to find it."

Charlotte made a lot of sense. She tended to be more levelheaded when I got frustrated and worried that one of my plans wasn't working out exactly as it should have.

I nodded. "You're right. We have to keep Driscoll away. Let's go."

CHAPTER 10

$\mathcal{W}$e propped the digger up so the blades wouldn't be resting on the ground. It may have been an unnecessary precaution considering the steel they'd been forged from, but I wasn't so sure about the mount of the blade itself.

"We used it to dig ore out of a rock wall," Charlotte said. "I'm sure it can survive sitting on the ground."

"Probably," I said, "but I'd rather not take the chance."

We finished clearing out the leather sacks we used for hiking and started dragging the wagon back up the ramp. The harness I had fastened around my shoulders and waist had actually been one of Theodore's ideas. Before that, we'd been dragging the wagon by hand, and every trip had been exhausting. I wouldn't say that hauling a load of ore was easy, but a great deal of strain had certainly been lifted by Theodore's addition.

"The question now," I said, taking a deep breath as we reached the top of the mine once more, "is whether or not Driscoll is waiting for us."

"Check your armor," Charlotte said. "We don't want to be caught unprepared."

I nodded and went about doing just that.

We reached the entrance to the mine, and I frowned at the overarching barrier of iron. I silently hoped we wouldn't need our armor, and stepped outside.

I dragged the wagon deeper into the waterfall, until we were nearly out the other side. This was the best place I'd found to lower the wagon into the waters. I undid the harness and pulled one of the sacks of ore onto my back. It was heavy, but not unbearably so. Charlotte did the same. Once we had a good length of rope tied to the edge of the wagon, Charlotte started back along the ridge. I slowly let the wagon slide into the waters, grinding my teeth as the corner went under, and blowing out a breath when the ballast tanks dipped for only a moment, keeping the wagon afloat. It vanished through the edge of the falls as Charlotte pulled it toward the other side.

I yanked the harmonica pistol out of my jacket and removed the ammunition from my vest. The two pieces slid together with a click, and I hurried around the bank to meet Charlotte.

She dragged the wagon through the water, maneuvering around boulders and small whirlpools until she finally reached the sloping bank we could use as a ramp on the other side.

"You have it?" I asked.

The look on her face told me that she had it, and that I was, in fact, an idiot for asking. Old habits, I supposed. You work with an apprentice long enough, and you just assume everyone needs a little help.

Charlotte had the wagon out of the water before she let out a long sigh. She slid the pack off her back and let the stone-filled leather crack down onto the small pile of ore. I did the same, awkwardly shifting the straps around my harmonica pistol.

"Did you see something?" Charlotte asked, eyeing the pistol.

I shook my head. "I don't want to fumble with it if I do see something. Just wanted to be ready."

Charlotte tapped the dark gray box on her vambrace. It was her way of telling me she agreed, without actually telling me she agreed.

I fastened the harness to myself again, and we started back down the trail. For the steeper parts of the woods, Charlotte pulled on the rope from behind to keep the wagon of ore from running me over. It was a little awkward in the rougher areas of the trail, and for the most severe parts, we both got behind the wagon. There were a lot of stupid ways to die in the woods, and getting run down by an ore wagon was particularly dumb.

I stared at the shadows to the west. The sun was high enough now that a decent amount of sunlight penetrated the canopy, but the shadows it cast were misleading at best. Every crack of a branch sent my eyes roaming toward the deepest parts of the woods. Charlotte studied the canopy, something you needed to do when you were dealing with an enemy that could fly.

"What's Driscoll's issue with this town anyway?" Charlotte asked. "Is it really just because he's at odds with the Court of the Sun and the Moon?"

"Around here, that's like saying is he really just at odds with the sheriff," I said. "Going against the rule of law in any city is bound to get you in trouble."

"Of course," Charlotte said. "That's why you have a license to produce liquor. All your moonshining is aboveboard."

"Of course," I said with a small laugh.

A twig snapped nearby, and I froze. Something was close, something big.

"You need not fear me, Gregory," a voice said from the shadows, so smooth and silky that I distrusted it immediately.

I started to unhook my pistol from my vest, but Charlotte's hand shot out and interrupted me.

"It's Orna," she said.

"The wood elf?"

The shadow of a tree moved, and a large deer strode into the clearing, and upon its back sat a creature of impossible beauty.

"Orna . . ." Charlotte whispered.

"Orna?" I said, raising my eyebrows.

"Peace, mortals," the woman said, her voice lilting as if sung by the finest bard, the sunlight caressing alabaster skin that betrayed no human imperfections.

"What do you want of us?" I asked, my voice throaty and gruff compared to Orna's.

"I have driven away the Unseelie stalking you in these woods. You bring my goddaughter into danger."

"Goddaughter?" I said, unable to keep the surprise from my voice.

"Betsy?" Charlotte asked.

Orna inclined her head. The deer moved with her, as if it too agreed with Charlotte's words.

"Yes, Betsy is the name she has taken for herself in this life. The name she has chosen to share with the mortals. No harm will come to her."

"We would never," I said.

"I do not believe you would intentionally harm her, or allow harm to come to her, but now comes the Unseelie known as Driscoll. And that is an unfortunate turn of events. Should my family come to harm from your meddling, I will hold you and Driscoll responsible. The consequences will be immediate."

"Betsy is her own person," Charlotte said as Orna started to turn away. "We don't control her decisions. Her willingness to help us was a kindness. But it does not place the responsibility on our shoulders."

Orna paused and tilted her head, slowly turning back to

Charlotte. "I have lived through days where I would have struck you down for such words. And perhaps there is some truth in your words, mortal. But there is more truth in mine. You will be held responsible."

Orna turned in earnest, and the deer began to pace away.

"Then help her," I shouted after her. "Stop Driscoll. Is it not your duty to stand against the Unseelie?"

She didn't turn around again, but her voice echoed through the woods and whispered through the leaves. "You have much to learn of the fae."

The deer crossed into a shadow, and Orna was gone.

Charlotte took a deep breath and turned to me. "That was new. What did we get tied up in this time?"

"Nothing much. Apparently just a minor fae who rules over the woods in this area. Still better than morgens."

Charlotte barked out a laugh. "Let's get back. The longer we stay here, the more likely it is Driscoll will come back."

I nodded and leaned into the harness.

CHAPTER 11

*H*eading back into the town was truly a relief. We dragged the wagon to the back of the shop, and I pulled up a small lift we'd installed on the rear deck. Footsteps sounded in the kitchen before the door creaked open.

"We were getting worried," Theodore said. "You've been gone quite a while."

I glanced at my watch and frowned at Theodore. "We've been up to the mine, acquired the ore, and journeyed back to town. I rather think we made excellent time."

"Did you see Driscoll?" Betsy asked as we crossed the threshold into the shop.

"We did," I said. "Thankfully, we lost him at the entrance to the mine. Although I'd say that was one of the less interesting parts of our trip."

"I saw him in town, too," Betsy said. "Walking toward the conservatory."

"If you saw him," Charlotte said, "it's because he wanted you to see him."

I nodded my agreement. "Boilers ready?"

Theodore nodded. "They're set, and the rock crushers are ready to go."

"Good," I said. "Start loading the ore in. As soon as you have it sorted out, get it in the crucible. We're going to try casting the vessels. We don't have time to form them by hand."

"Time before what?" Betsy asked.

"Time before Driscoll comes after you, and then your godmother comes after us."

"What?" she said, unable to conceal the surprise in her voice.

"The more interesting part of our trip," Charlotte said.

"You saw Orna?" Theodore asked.

I smiled. "You've been sharing a lot with him."

"That's none of your business," Betsy said. "It's none of hers, either."

"I'll be sure to remember that when she tramples us with her *deer*," Charlotte snapped.

"You're welcome here," I said, "but the least you can do is forewarn us."

"How am I supposed to forewarn you of something I'm unaware of?" Betsy snapped. "Most of the fae won't intercede in mortal affairs, but you can rest assured they'll take revenge. They thrive on it."

Theodore, apparently being the wiser of the two of us in that moment, dragged the wagon back through the kitchen and out into the workshop where the crucible and the rock crusher waited.

"Perfect—" I started.

"Shut it," Charlotte said. Her voice was just as cutting as Betsy's, only I didn't understand where the anger was coming from. "Leave her alone. She's good as family to us, as much as Theodore is, and I'll not have you talking down to her."

My anger flared for a moment, but I stifled it with a deep

breath. Charlotte was right. Betsy was sticking her neck out for Theodore, for us. How could we do any less?

I ground my teeth together and slid out of my tool-laden vest. I let it drop with a loud thud to the workbench as I stormed through the doorway, more angry with myself than Betsy. "I'm sorry."

As I followed Theodore out into our second workshop, I heard Charlotte telling Betsy that I didn't always handle stress very well. She was right, but the comment rankled.

The workshop in the back of the building wasn't as neat and polished as the workbenches that the customers saw. Here there was almost always a fine layer of dust on things, but it wasn't from lack of use. It was the powder created from pulverizing rock, along with shards left from working with glass and metal. The scent of hot metal and burning coals filled the air, the small steam engine whirring as it pumped air into the fires.

The shop felt like home. Sometimes even more so than the home we kept above it.

"You okay?" Theodore asked.

I nodded. I picked up some of the larger chunks of ore and placed them in the chute of the rock crusher. The metal and stone clanged against the steel slide.

Theodore pulled the brass lever down that opened the gate for the steam. The piston started up, bits of ore rattling into the crusher as our conversation was drowned out by the calamity of the machine.

We continued like that for a few moments, feeding the raw ore into the machine and gathering the crushed remnants on the other side.

There it mixed with water before running down a sluice. The concentrate separated until we were left with rock containing the metals we needed, and a lighter, more fluid mass that carried smaller flecks and shards of the gray substance. Theodore funneled this into a barrel. Once we had enough, he loaded the smaller remnants onto the wagon with the barrel and dragged it toward the back door.

I turned to watch him go before starting to shut down the rock crusher. It would take a while for heat from the steam engine to dissipate. In the meantime, we could start smelting the ore.

Once I was satisfied the fires were out and the rock crusher was on its way to cooling down, I followed Theodore into the back.

The furnace may have been attached to the shop, but it generated far too much heat to keep it indoors. Perhaps it would've been possible if we had a large barn, or other open area, but as it was, I didn't want to burn the house down.

Theodore flipped open the metal disc that sat on top of the furnace. Inside burned a fire hot enough that it glowed like the sun.

The long tongs we used for loading ore into the crucible were unwieldy and hard to handle. I'd come up with a solution to use it with wicker baskets. We lowered it into the crucible where it burst into flames and let the ore settle to the bottom.

"We can get more in here," Theodore said. "Probably at least another quarter of the load."

I shook my head. "We don't need that much."

I grabbed a hook and used it to pull the heavy lid closed. Theodore turned the valve, and airflow into the furnace increased, sending a small burst of flame out through the hole in the center of the lid.

"You want to do anything with the barrel now?" Theodore asked.

"No," I said. "We have all we need for the vessels. Let's focus on that."

"How do you plan to cast these?" Theodore asked.

Most of the work we'd done with the vessels for the aether

involved crafting them by hand. That took time, more time than I was willing to risk with Driscoll in town.

I pulled two pairs of wood blocks out from underneath the workbench beside the furnace.

"You can't get the details of the vessels chamber with that," Theodore said.

I handed Theodore one set of blocks and said, "Look inside."

Theodore cracked the block open, and his eyes widened as he stared at the intricate web work of copper and iron. "You think this will work?"

"The theory is sound. And what better time than now to test it?"

"I don't know," Theodore said. "Maybe about two weeks ago before we really needed it?"

I barked out a harsh laugh and said, "You make a fair point. Ore from the cave will form a bond with the copper."

"An alloy," Theodore said, nodding his head. "And the iron has a higher melting point so it should help you keep it shaped."

"That's the theory," I said.

"Aren't you worried about weakening the wards?" Betsy asked as she stepped outside the shop and joined us by the furnace.

I glanced between her and Theodore before nodding. "Do you think it will impair the aether itself?"

Betsy frowned. "I honestly don't know. The vessel you're building, it is not a solid structure."

"I'm hoping the alloy will have enough of the ore's property to conduct the aether."

Betsy nodded. "I suppose we'll see soon enough."

"Let's get them ready," I said.

Theodore put the mold back together, and set it into a square metal box partially filled with sand. I handed him the second mold, and he did the same.

"You think those channels are wide enough to take the alloy?" he asked as he studied the points we'd be pouring the molten metal into.

"Should be fine," I said. "Let's fill that up with sand and get ready to pour."

Betsy studied the furnace and the box we were using to cast the vessels. "I think I'll just wait inside."

I leaned toward Theodore. "I think she's smarter than us."

"Oh, I have no doubt about that," Theodore said.

The door clicked closed behind Betsy as Theodore finished leveling the sand off around the molds.

"Grab the tongs," I said as I picked up the hook and moved toward the furnace.

"You want me to pour?" Theodore asked.

"I can handle this." I pulled on thick heavy leather gloves. The padding inside of them was enough that I could barely move my hands, but it provided an adequate level of insulation from the heat of the forge.

Theodore hurried to put his own gloves on. Once he was ready, I lowered the end into the forge, and hooked the tongs around the crucible.

"Locked in," I said.

"Ready."

He nodded and stepped back, only helping with leverage to get the crucible, now filled with slag and molten ore, evenly out of the forge. Even with our protective clothes on, this wasn't the kind of thing you wanted sloshing over your feet. I'd known more than one blacksmith over the years who had terrible injuries from accidents like that. I'd known some who didn't survive it.

Sweat poured off both of us as the heat of the open furnace filled the area with a stifling blast of air. I positioned the red-hot crucible in the sand and took a deep breath before turning my entire body slightly to line up the spout on the crucible with the opening in the mold. Another moment of focus, and then I levered it forward. Liquid metal slid from the crucible like a river of heated butter. It spat steam into the air as it slid into the mold. It only took a few seconds of pouring before the opening at the other end of the mold bubbled molten metal up in the sandbox. I carefully tilted the crucible back into a sitting position.

"Let's get the other one," I said, grabbing the tongs close to where they were connected. I could feel the heat through my gloves now, a good sign that I was done handling the tongs. With the crucible positioned, Theodore stepped away. I repeated the pour before emptying the crucible into a small round pocket at the edge of the metal box. Once the extra metal cooled, we could knock the slag off and would have all the metal we needed to make the rest of the vessels later.

CHAPTER 12

"Turn the forge down," I said. "We shouldn't need it now."

Theodore stuck the crucible back on top of the forge before he released the tongs. Those he hung back on the metal hooks, with the heat safely out of the way.

Theodore straightened his back with a start and turned to face me. "Are we going to get aether in those?"

"It's already in," I said. "It's the only option I could think of that would allow us to do the casting."

Theodore looked back at the box of molds. "What if it would've ruptured?"

"I suppose if it had, we likely wouldn't be talking about it right now."

"If this works," Betsy said, walking back outside to join us, "you've only provided the town protection against one threat. I don't believe these wards will dissuade a great many of the other things that threaten the settlement."

"And I thought I was the optimistic one," I said.

Charlotte let out a low laugh as she followed Betsy out the back door. "The biggest threat to this place right now is Driscoll," Charlotte said. "Whether the people who live here know it or not."

Betsy nodded. "There's more you don't know. Driscoll is Unseelie, clearly, and he wears that fact proudly. What you don't know is that he is vile even by the standards of the Unseelie fae. Many years ago, Driscoll's sister was exiled from this place. A faerie of the wood, exiled to the desert. You understand what that means?"

I exchanged a look with Charlotte. I had some idea of what the consequences might have been, but not enough.

"No," I said.

Charlotte shook her head too.

"It is a slow death," Betsy said. "Taken away from the magicks that sustained her, she would have starved. Some of the old tales say it took months, and some say it took years. But there's one thing all of the stories agree on. Driscoll found her before she died, but he was too late. He may not be at odds with the Court of the Sun and the Moon directly, but he is at odds with anyone who trespasses on the land where his sister lived. The mere existence of this town has awakened a monster that you do not understand. And that monster knows what you did to the Unseelie fae of the Caribbean."

"We get the wards in place," I said. "That's our priority."

"He's had time to study the conservatory," Charlotte said. "He's seen the wards work. He likely already knows what we're doing."

I looked down at the molds at our feet. "He might know, but he'll be too late to stop us."

The molten metals cooled quite quickly once they were in the mold. Without the heat of the forge to keep the temperatures above the melting point, the metal regained its form in moments. It wouldn't be cool enough to touch with bare hands until we quenched it.

"What do you want to do?" Theodore asked. "Drop them straight in the bucket? Or crack the molds and inspect them first?"

"Just drop them right in the buckets. We don't have the time to worry about small imperfections in the castings right now. There's no point in inspecting them too closely."

Theodore nodded.

I picked up the wooden block with my padded leather gloves, undid the small clamp holding the two halves closed, and let the vessel inside fall into the water. It hissed, and steam exploded from the top of the bucket as the metal sank to the bottom. Theodore did the same, and we waited for the frenzy of activity to slow. The boiling waters became a slow stream of bubbles as the steam cleared enough we could see the bottom of the steel bucket.

I reached in with a short pair of tongs and grasped the first of the vessels. I held up a small cylinder and frowned at the coloration. The webwork of copper we'd used to frame everything out had held up fairly well, but as it melted, it created something that almost looked more like Damascus steel than the uniform coloration of the vessels we'd crafted by hand.

"It looks good," I said. "It should be functional. But give it a few more minutes to cool down, and we can try it in one of the wards."

"So soon?" Theodore asked.

"Yes. I doubt that aether would be affected very much by letting it cool down more. If it wasn't destroyed in the mold, it should be working."

"Let me see it," Betsy said.

I held the tongs out to her, but instead of taking them from me, she plucked the vessel off the end before I could so much as shout a warning about the heat.

I blinked at her.

She rubbed at the gray and copper cylinder.

"Wow," I said, watching as she cleared the soot and remnants away. Beneath was a brilliantly polished core.

"I can still sense the aether," she said. "But it is odd. I sense it as if it is a blankness. As if it has dulled my senses. I don't know if I will ever grow accustomed to that sensation."

I frowned. "I don't want these wards to affect you. I want them to affect the Unseelie. Are you sure you'll be okay when we activate this web of wards?"

Betsy nodded. "The aether in this vessel has no purpose. The wards give it purpose. My family has used wards similar to those for many years. We will be safe."

"One day you're going to tell us how many years," Charlotte said, crossing her arms.

Betsy gave her a small smile before holding the vessel back out to me.

"Is it safe to touch?"

"What he means," Charlotte said, "is it safe for him to touch?"

Betsy released a small laugh and nodded.

I took the vessel from her outstretched hand and felt the warmth rising in my palm. It was not too hot, and the temperature evened out just before it reached uncomfortable levels.

Charlotte stepped closer and studied the vessel in my hand. "It's beautiful."

"I didn't expect that," I said.

"Get the gun," she said, looking into my eyes.

I nodded. "Theodore, it's time for us to test this."

"Finally!" Theodore said, hurrying into the shop.

"I only hope we won't need to use it," I said.

Betsy took a deep breath. "That is a noble thought. But Driscoll is fond of threes. He will not come alone."

CHAPTER 13

The heavy clank from inside the workshop told me Theodore had opened one of the safes. It was an odd thing to work on something for so long without testing it.

"We came here to escape this life," Charlotte said.

I grimaced and took the oak case from Theodore. "No rest for the wicked."

I set the case on the workbench near the forge and threw the latch to open it. The hinges were whisper quiet, and they gave up their contents without protest. Inside was a nest of leather and velvet and steel.

An oddly shaped gun waited in the beautiful case Charlotte had made for it. Of all the things I'd thought to do with the aether, I must confess, I didn't expect it to be crafted into a weapon.

"Pirate stories again?" Theodore asked.

"I don't believe that was a story," Betsy said. "There is much truth in Gregory's words, and Charlotte's."

I ran my finger down the bronze inlays on the side of the pistol. At first glance, one might think it was just a contemporary revolver, but it was far more than that. I slid the polished cylinder out and frowned at the single hole drilled inside it.

"Pass me the vessel," I said. I knew I'd been lucky to only lose one still since we discovered the aether. Theodore's mistake was one that I'd made myself, unaware of the power hidden in those waters. I hadn't told him just how lucky he was. And now we were casting the stuff in fire and metal.

Theodore sanded off the last vestige of the mold we used to cast the new vessel. I took it from him gently and slid it into the cylinder before closing the gun.

Betsy cursed when the small glass window on the top of the barrel began to glow, dim at first, but increasing until it became as bright as one of the lanterns the townsfolk would carry at night.

"Not particularly stealthy," Charlotte said.

"It doesn't need to be," I said. "It only needs to kill a fae."

"You're telling me you were pirates?" Theodore asked.

I placed my thumb in an indentation beneath the barrel and drew it back slowly. About the time the movement reached the cylinder, a satisfying click sounded.

"There aren't real pirates anymore," I said. "They're dead or imprisoned."

"We're just shopkeepers and moonshiners now," Charlotte said.

Theodore narrowed his eyes.

"They've killed fae before," Betsy said.

"And we'll kill them again," I said, leveling the pistol at a thick area of scrub brush. I moved my finger to the trigger and let the hammer drop. A narrow beam of light rocketed out of the end of the gun, leaving no recoil in my hand but a strange feeling in my heart as I stared at the smoking ruin of the bush.

"Shit," I muttered, frowning at the weapon in my hand. I crouched and studied the bush. The damage that beam had done to the wood was terrifying. It had cut a hole clean through it. The aether gun wasn't something I'd want in an enemy's hands.

Charlotte rubbed at her ear. "Not as loud as a pistol, but that whine was one strange sound."

"I think the more important fact," I said, "is that we're not all dead."

Betsy pinched the bridge of her nose. "Humans. It's a wonder you live as long as you do."

"Do you have any weapons?" I asked.

"Of course," she said. "Half human, so only half an idiot."

Charlotte grinned at Betsy while Theodore awkwardly shuffled his feet.

"Still coming to terms with this whole thing?" Charlotte asked.

"It's fine," Theodore said. "She's just never been this open about it with other people. It's . . . odd."

"I get it," I said. "It's a big secret that only the two of you have known as long as you've been together. And now we know. It changes things."

"It changes nothing," Betsy said. "I will be with Theodore as long as he needs me, or until he dies. It is as simple as that."

"I felt much the same way about a cat I once had," I said.

Theodore's anxiousness fractured into a smile. "Shut up, old man."

"Get your armor, your shotgun, and whatever iron-rich blades you have laying around."

"Here we go," Charlotte said. "Now he's going to say we're going to stop Driscoll here or die trying."

I blinked. "That's absolutely not what I was going to say."

"Uh huh."

"Dammit, woman," I grumbled.

"Told you," Charlotte said, turning to Theodore. "Get your supplies. We have to hurry."

"We must seal the last two wards before Driscoll can destroy the mounts," Betsy said. "If he saw what you've done at the conservatory, he may now know what he's looking for."

"Then like Charlotte said," I said, "hurry."

I studied the holster that Charlotte had strapped to her waist. The aether gun fit neatly into the old cracked leather. I smiled at her.

Charlotte pulled a thin shawl over her shoulders. It hung low enough to conceal the guns, but it still left her vambrace exposed. Normally I'd consider that an issue, but today it could mean the difference between life and death.

The thought of the sleeve or some other piece of clothing getting caught on that vambrace and slowing down one of the iron bolts that weapon could throw was sobering at best. It was always good to think positive before battle, but I'd never been able to convince my brain to do that. I always thought of what could go wrong, what we could plan for, and what we could fall back on.

That paranoia may have been why we were still around. We'd spent time at sea, as what some would call pirates, and Charlotte and I had survived more than one battle. Engagements at sea were different. You were less likely to be surrounded, and it was easier to tell where your enemies were headed. Chances were, they were either trying to sink your ship, or board it and take it.

But now we were in a town. Surrounded by wilderness on all sides. Many different people had come here for various reasons. But that wasn't my real concern. On land, it was harder to find your enemies' target, unless you yourself were that target. We suspected Driscoll was trying to stop our placement of the wards. But we didn't know for sure.

But if we were right, that could mean one of Betsy's friends, or even her fae family, could have let slip the nature of our work. But what if it wasn't someone from her family? What if it was someone who was already seated in the Court of the Sun and the Moon?

"Bishop," I said, turning to Betsy as she came back down the stairs with Theodore. "Did you tell Bishop?"

"About Driscoll?" Betsy asked. "No."

I frowned and looked away. "How else could Bishop know? Who else would've told him?"

"That's neither here nor there," Charlotte said. "Stop your worrying and straighten your back."

I pulled my vest closed and double checked the clasps on my vambrace. As I had the harmonica pistol, I kept the shield cartridge loaded on my wrist. Charlotte opted for the bolt thrower, but she was always more mindful of offense than defense.

Once I was satisfied I had everything locked down, and had dropped the remaining vessels into the pouch at my waist, I made for the back door. "Let's get this done."

We walked out of the back of the shop, the entire time Betsy's warning about Driscoll preferring threes echoing in my mind. I led the group south to Main Street. It had been a long day, and I doubted we would have sunlight for more than a couple more hours.

The streets were busier now, both with workers hammering away in some of the newer buildings and those local residents who had been here since the town was founded not so long ago. We headed east, along the same road that would take us to the inn, only that wasn't our destination that evening.

Or at least not our first destination.

One thing every town needed was a saloon, and our small town hidden in the wilderness of the Colorado territory was no different. People liked to joke that the saloon was the first building to go up when the settlement first started, but it wasn't really a joke. It literally had been one of the first buildings to be erected.

It was also where we met the first of our opposition.

CHAPTER 14

"**T**inker," the slender face said as its owner stepped off the wooden deck and onto the gravel street. "We have business."

"He's my business," Betsy said. "If you take issue with that, you can speak with the Court."

The newcomer bared his teeth, contorting his face into a rictus grin that looked anything but human.

"Gregory and Charlotte Trent," the faerie said. "You carry with you a power that does not belong to humans."

"It's distilled from the power of witches," Charlotte said. "It is the very power of humans."

The fae curled his lip and looked down at Charlotte. He stood close to a foot taller than my wife, and nearly that much taller than me, but Charlotte didn't back down. She stared the fae down as her fingers traced the outline of her vambrace.

"Your reputation precedes you," he said with a small inclination of his head. "I am Cathal, brother to Driscoll and seeker of stolen magicks."

"It's my right to protect my home," I said. "It's every one of our rights. Now step aside."

"You are a fool," Cathal said with a humorless laugh. "You do not sail upon a galleon in the seas to the south. You are not armed with mighty iron cannons, loaded and prepared to do battle with the morgens. What hope have you?"

"Theodore, take him," I said.

"No!" Betsy said. Whether she'd meant to issue a warning, or something else, it came too late.

The weapon Theodore wielded looked like a crossbow to those not familiar with it. It worked much the same, but it had the ability to fire three bolts at once. Hit a man in the chest with that, and he'd rarely get back up. Hit a fae in the chest with three iron bolts, and he'd die screaming.

Cathal barely raised his right arm, causing the fabric of his sleeve to billow out and catch the iron bolts. In one violent motion, he snapped his arm downward, and the bolts clanged against the gravel.

"Fool," Cathal muttered. "You think every fae in this town hasn't heard of your inventions? You think the fae of the Caribbean would not tell of your slaughter of the morgens? We will have your blood for theirs."

I almost growled. Cathal knew more of our history than I would've suspected. He knew more of it than Theodore knew, which meant at least some of his knowledge hadn't come from Betsy, and I let that small sliver of trust I had in her grow just a little more.

Cathal stepped toward Theodore, continuing his diatribe as he drew a slender blade sheathed at his waist. I hesitated to call it a dagger, but it wasn't quite long enough to be a short sword. The weight of the harmonica pistol felt good in my grasp. I'd been in enough firefights to learn how to control my movements, even when our lives were on the line.

The cartridge slid home with a satisfying click, and I raised the barrel. There was a time when I was more noble and I probably would've warned Cathal, but I'd grown impatient in my old age. Or perhaps I'd grown more cautious.

I pulled the trigger smoothly, and the light from the ward on the clip shone almost as bright as the burst of fire from the end of the gun. It was a good shot, taking Cathal in the shoulder. But where the iron should have crashed into his body and sent him to the earth, instead it ricocheted off into the air.

The fae looked back at me, his eyes wide before he dashed behind Theodore and I lost my shot. I expected the fae to take Theodore hostage, but instead he sprinted past us, dodging behind a carriage full of wary onlookers.

"He ran," Betsy said, the disbelief plain in her voice.

I stared after him. He was fast and moved with a sublime grace that I only saw in the supernatural creatures I'd encountered, and extremely seasoned fighters. "He could've taken us."

The world shimmered, and Cathal vanished. It was as if a thin veil of water had run across my vision, and then it was gone.

"What the hell was that?" Charlotte asked.

"A misdirection," Betsy said. "He can hide himself through magic. It's a skill some of the older fae have. I'm surprised you didn't encounter it when you battled the morgens in the Caribbean."

I frowned. "We've seen similar things, but nothing quite so comprehensive. I could've sworn his very footsteps vanished."

Betsy shook her head. "That's unlikely. Too many sounds for him to mask at once. And here," she said, gesturing to the calm crowds walking around us, "it would appear he hid our altercation from the townsfolk."

"Fine," Theodore said. "Gregory and Charlotte are pirates, and crazed fae are trying to kill us. Why don't we stop thinking about it and hurry up to get the shit done?"

"Theodore's right," I said, hurrying toward the back of the saloon and rummaging through a pocket on my vest. I pulled a pair of goggles over my eyes and clipped an aether lens to the side. I glanced at Charlotte. "Why didn't you take a shot?"

"And tip our hand so early?" she asked. "You're smarter than that, dear."

I gave a sharp nod and focused on the saloon. While the other buildings we were warding were still under construction, or at least repair, the saloon had already been here. And since I didn't really know where everyone's loyalties lied, I didn't dare tell the proprietors what we were doing. That meant the ward for the saloon needed to be installed outside, or we would have to break in. Certainly a possibility, but also a good way to get killed.

Sixteen across and four down, I counted to myself as I ran my hand along the bricks. At the end, there waited a brick where the mortar had been chipped away. We'd wedged a bit of painted wood into the gap that was textured to look like mortar. It would decay faster than the actual stone, but to the casual observer, it was virtually identical.

I cursed when I realized the new rain barrel that had been placed out back was slightly in the way. "Help me move this."

Theodore came around to my side of the barrel. He put his shoulder into the edge while I twisted at the top. We didn't need to move it far, but even half a foot made quite a ruckus. Once we were done kicking up dust and grunting with the effort, I took a deep breath and looked around. I was happy to find no one had their attention on us.

I stuck the edge of the metal bar into the groove that should've been mortar. I wiggled it around a bit, the metal scraping and squealing against the brick before the wood gave way. I grasped it between my fingernails and pulled. The brick behind it fell into a slant, and Charlotte pulled it out before I turned back. I grabbed the second brick from on top of it and one from beside it to reveal the mount we'd installed in the wall.

"It's not going to work as well as the pipes in the conservatory," Betsy said.

"Just watch our backs," I said. "We'll deal with it if it fails."

Theodore rummaged through the leather sack he'd had on his back. He pulled out one of the pipe-mounted wards, very much like what we had installed at the conservatory.

"Slide it in," I said. "Keep the narrow end to the east."

Theodore glanced up and frowned.

"Pointed at me," I said.

Theodore nodded and leaned forward.

"Hold it steady," I said as I docked the pipe. Once it was stable, I pulled the small lever hidden behind one of the mortared bricks. It clicked and sent the gears turning, which caused the small piston to slide into the top of the ward. I nodded in satisfaction as the plates slowly spread out.

"Looks good," Charlotte said. The last segment of the plate expanded, and the ward glowed. Something crashed inside the saloon. Loud enough I could hear through the wall, and large enough I could feel it in the bricks as I slid everything back together.

"Sounds like we may have surprised some fae inside the saloon," Betsy said.

"Let's move," Charlotte said. "If that's what happened, we don't need to be out here when they come to investigate."

We shifted the barrel back, and Charlotte kicked at the dirt to hide the signs that anyone had moved it. We hurried to the east and rounded the corner of the block before I heard raised voices behind us.

"Get onto the street," Charlotte said. We crossed over the square, and it was a straight shot to the meeting hall.

We were halfway across the square before anyone really noticed us.

"I'm sure that's them," someone said from behind us.

"They look busy," someone else said. "Let's just leave them alone."

I glanced back and saw some of our recent customers. Charlotte caught me looking, and our entire group slowed down. She turned to face whatever was behind us, her hand sliding toward her vambrace.

I gave a tiny shake of my head, and her hand fell away.

"Oh, we didn't mean to bother you," the woman behind us said.

"We just wanted to thank you for the beautiful puzzle box," the man said.

"It's no trouble, dears," Charlotte said. "We're just looking for one of our friends, and I am afraid we don't have much time to talk. But I appreciate you telling us. It was very kind of you."

"Of course," the man said. "Thank you again."

I inclined my head as we parted ways. "What was their name again?"

"You are terrible with names, Gregory," Charlotte said.

"Almost as bad as Theodore," Betsy said. "That was Lawrence and his wife, Christine. Come now. We must hurry."

Apparently our hurried manner was enough to turn away the usually polite townsfolk. The crunch of gravel in the center of the town square gave way to a patch of grass. Our footsteps fell quiet until we reached the next street, and the meeting hall.

The core of the building was simple enough, but that wasn't my focus. That wasn't our goal. On either side of the squat building rose the framing of a beautiful expansion. By the time they had the meeting hall completed, it would rival some of the nicest buildings I'd seen in my travels.

"Come," I said, "to the left. Down the alley, and we're nearly there."

The alley was a narrow thing, not so much due to its own nature, but due to the fact they had stacked lumber and various building supplies all along it. Once we cleared the edge, and the walls were open, we stepped into the skeleton of the new construction.

Once we were on the north side of the meeting hall, we were in the shadow of what many called Mount Alexa. Something about the woods on the north side of the town always unsettled me. It was an odd thing, as technically the woods where my still resided was in the Northwoods, but it was nothing like that looming form of Mount Alexa. Perhaps it was Orna, ever keeping a watchful eye. Or perhaps it was something more ominous, something we mortals couldn't understand, and maybe never would.

We wove between the precisely cut wooden supports of the new expansion. It wasn't the wood that interested me. It was the massive iron beams they'd used as the main supports. It gave me pause, knowing that a building that would harbor fae intermittently would be partially constructed of iron. Perhaps it had been intentional? I couldn't say, but it would work for my purposes.

"Here," I said, kneeling down near the center of the rear construction. The middle of the iron column had what appeared to be a welded plate over it. But that wasn't it at all. While I had made the cuts at the conservatory, I'd recruited Theodore to prepare the installation at the meeting hall.

Our packs thumped down onto the hardened earth beneath the black iron. Theodore opened his pack and pulled out the last of the wards. This one was different. Much as we'd customized the others to fit the bronze pipework in the conservatory and the brass piston we'd installed in the saloon, this one was a darker affair. The post was nearly solid iron, while the plate that hosted the wards was an alloy.

I placed a magnet in the center of the welded plate. The response was instant. I could hear the bolt retract as the magnet pulled on the levers behind the plate. It was delicate work, getting the gears in the proper ratio that a simple magnet could undo the bolts, but Theodore had proven his skill.

I pulled the plate off with ease. Charlotte took it out of my hand while Theodore reached into the void. He settled the bottom of the post onto a slightly raised bolt. It fit squarely in the socket on the base of the ward, and one hard push locked the top of it into place. I slid one long locking pin from the front through the back before reaching behind the assembly and bending the pin down.

"You're sure that's enough to hold it?" Theodore asked.

I fished around in the pocket on my vest and pulled out the last of our new vessels. "I suppose we'll know in a second."

I pulled the spring-loaded panel to the side on the post before sliding the vessel inside. I let the panel snap closed, and a moment later the plate sprang into action. Each segment locked into the one before it until it fully formed the ward and started to glow.

"So far, so good," Charlotte said.

"Why do you always have to say that?" I asked. "Every time."

"Oh, come now," Charlotte said. "Put your silly superstitions to rest. Nothing bad has happened since we retired."

"Retired from being a pirate?" Theodore muttered.

I stared at the ward. And waited.

And waited.

"I don't sense the wards connecting," Betsy said.

"Every. Time," I said as I looked up at Charlotte.

"Check it again," Theodore said. "Is it in right?"

I gave him a flat look.

"We need to get back to the conservatory," Betsy said, wringing her hands. "Driscoll was there earlier."

I cursed. "What if he got to the ward?"

Charlotte bit her lip and shook her head. "No, he can't touch it."

"We need to get back there," Betsy said. "Now."

I took a deep breath and closed my eyes, willing myself to calm down. She was right. We needed to get back to the conservatory and see what had been compromised. There couldn't be another explanation, unless the wards themselves had failed, and I couldn't afford that kind of doubt.

I gave one sharp nod and hopped up to my feet. "Grab your bags. We're going."

CHAPTER 15

*T*heodore tied the flap of his backpack off and slung it over his shoulder. I followed suit, the sweat on my palms causing the leather to grow slick beneath my grasp.

We hurried out the back of the meeting hall construction, hurdling supplies and ducking through the various supports of the new construction.

Once we were out on the road behind it, more of a dirt path really, I started to notice more of the sounds in the city. In the distance you could just barely hear the falls crashing, and I realized it wasn't so much the sounds of the city I was hearing, but the lack of sound.

We hurried east until we reached the edge of the meeting hall, and then we cut south. Charlotte took the lead, as she had always been the lookout when we were on the seas. While my vision had grown worse with age, to the point that I could barely get around without some sort of glasses, she could still spot prey at two hundred yards.

Theodore and Betsy stayed close behind us as our speed increased. The silence bothered me, and the farther we made it through the town square, the more I realized just how quiet it was.

"What's going on?" I asked, my gaze flashing from Betsy back to Charlotte.

"They're waiting for us," Betsy said. "They've already masked the area from the locals. But this is beyond Driscoll's skill. I can still hear you, and you can still hear me. The discipline it would take to make a cloak like this so precise is astounding."

"You're not making me feel much better, girl," Charlotte said. She pulled a lever on the side of her vambrace, releasing the safety on the bolt thrower she now had mounted to it.

I unhooked the strap that was loosely holding the harmonica pistol against my chest. It would be a quick draw and easy aim, and I only hoped it would be fast enough.

We closed on the front of the inn, skirting around its grand façade. We stayed to the west of the building, hugging the wide porch and the turret that rose three stories above us. I glanced up at one of the brick chimneys that crowned the roof, and could've sworn I saw movement.

"Something's above us," I said.

Charlotte nodded, and I suspected she was the only one who had heard me. Once we cleared the side of the inn, the conservatory came into view.

"You'll not keep me from my prey, mortal," Driscoll said. His glare was icy enough to physically cut someone. If he'd been human, I would've said he looked cocky. But most fae I'd encountered over the years weren't the overconfident type. They generally knew what advantage they had, and how to leverage it.

"You here alone?" I asked.

"Only I stand before you," Driscoll said.

I'd once heard a tale that the fae told lies through truth, and I'd seen it and heard it with my own ears more than once. I turned my body slightly toward the inn and drew the harmonica pistol in one swift motion. The trigger clicked back, and the hammer dropped. The boom that followed would be enough to draw a crowd if the fae weren't masking everything we were doing.

But that hadn't been my point.

The shadow on the roof danced away from the bullet, and while I was quite sure no fae could move so fast as to dodge a bullet, the rapid motion of the blur certainly gave that impression. But I watched in satisfaction as one of the tiles beneath its foot slipped, and Cathal came tumbling down to the edge of the roof. With one violent swipe of his hand, he broke through the edge of the inn and grasped the hole he'd just created to keep from falling.

Cathal wasn't so slender as Driscoll. His chest was broader and tapered into a muscled waist. He looked down at me and snarled.

"What sorcery have you?" he shouted down. "No mortal can see us."

I let a small smile crawl over my face. I raised the aether magnifier away from the goggle over my left eye. "Apparently humans can do more than you know."

The faerie narrowed his eyes, released his grip, and thumped gracefully onto the earth not twenty feet from the barrel of my gun. "Can your lens protect you from a sword in your gut?"

Charlotte moved out to my right. It was a standard formation we'd used more than once when our ship had been boarded on the seas. I didn't care how good of a sailor you were, there was always a faster pirate, a stealthier ship, and you had to trust someone at your back.

Theodore had been a brawler before Betsy knocked some sense into him. He worked hard, but he'd also made a serious effort at screwing up his life. But it was the side of him that tended toward violence I hoped he'd brought today.

"Brothers," Betsy said. "Leave this place in peace."

"Halfbreed," Driscoll snarled. "Do not spew your talk of peace with me. These people have invaded our lands, people who are wanted by the very courts that govern us."

"He is my mate," Betsy said, stepping closer to Theodore. "You cannot strike him down, without breaking the very bonds of the fae. If you would strike at him, you strike at me."

"You speak of the old laws," Cathal said. "But you are a halfbreed. You have lived your entire life in the shadow of the mortals. You have no comprehension of what you speak."

"So be it," Betsy said. She drew a slender blade from each sleeve of her loose-fitting gown. "Leave now, or you will not leave this place alive."

"Fool."

"Found him," Theodore said. "Tree line to the east. Looks like a bow."

"What?" Driscoll said, his gaze turning to the trees.

Driscoll was almost as fast to turn as Charlotte was to draw the aether gun. The fae had never seen something like that, of that I had little doubt. The dim glow of the aether brightened as Charlotte pulled the mechanism below the barrel back in full. The fae in the woods had to have been a hundred yards away, no easy shot. But the bolt of magic that the aether gun threw had no concern for the wind in the air, or the friction of the barrel, or the head that it destroyed.

I couldn't hear the fae fall, but I could see the gore, and the collapse of the ruined body.

"You know not what you've done," Driscoll snarled as he drew his sword.

"Exterminating the bilge rats," Charlotte growled.

I expected him to talk more—that's usually how it went with the immortals. They fixated on spewing nonsense as they went about eviscerating their enemies. Driscoll had apparently spoken enough words. He moved like lightning, diving back into the webwork of the conservatory and dodging between the brass supports.

The other fae kept his gaze fixated on Charlotte's gun. I wasn't sure if he was tracking the barrel in order to make sure he didn't get his own head blown off, or if he was just lusting after the damned thing.

"How long?" I shouted.

"Less than half," Charlotte said.

I cursed under my breath. From what Charlotte was saying, the aether gun wouldn't be ready to fire for another minute at least. If I was being honest with myself, the two remaining fae could kill us all in that time. But they didn't know we couldn't fire again yet. They just thought we were half-crazed mortals. And that we could use to our advantage.

I pressed the plate on my vambrace, and the teardrop-shaped shield erupted on the back of my arm. It was one of the hardest alloys I'd ever seen, and Charlotte and I had put it up against gunfire and swords and a hundred different weapons. But here, faced with a half-mad fae, I worried just how much it could stop.

I sidestepped to the right, keeping the harmonica pistol leveled roughly between Cathal and Driscoll. They both kept the relaxed stance, which was both infuriating and intimidating. Charlotte and Theodore moved with me. I hadn't spent much time training Theodore on the finer points of strategic combat, and that was a fact I regretted in that moment.

"Theodore, don't!" Betsy shouted.

But Theodore was already moving, closing the distance between him and Cathal. A slow smile lifted the corners of Cathal's lips. I cursed, shifted my aim for Cathal, and fired. The harmonica pistol boomed, and the clip moved one more slot toward being empty. The bullet ricocheted into the air, hitting an invisible force not two inches from Cathal's shoulder. The faerie snarled and brought a rapid left uppercut into Theodore's ribs.

I didn't have to hear the crack to know something had broken. Theodore stumbled forward, aiming a clumsy left-handed blow at Cathal's face. The faerie reared back to strike again, but Theodore smacked the button on his vambrace, and a shield much like mine exploded around his arm. Except unlike mine, the boy had added some very nasty blades to the edge, the longest of which cut into the collarbone of the fae. Cathal roared in pain and spun away.

Driscoll's calm façade fractured, and he moved into action. Betsy broke formation, skirting past me and whispering in my ear, "Fix the ward."

She shoved off me, sending me stumbling toward Charlotte, and closer to the pipes where we'd installed the ward.

Charlotte aimed her wrist and clicked the button on her vambrace. Three bolts shot out, two finding nothing but air, but the third cutting into Driscoll's sleeve. The faerie doubled over, his smug expression completely overcome by the pain of the iron. He ripped his shirt sleeve off as he threw the projectile to the ground. In a motion so quick I could barely follow, the faerie tossed a throwing dagger at Charlotte. She barely had her arm up in time to stop the blade with her own flesh, but instead the razor-sharp projectile sank into the mechanism on her vambrace. There'd be no more bolts flying from that.

Betsy took the opportunity to aim a swift kick at Driscoll's head while Theodore wrestled with Cathal. Cathal grabbed Theodore and threw him to the ground, sending a cloud of dust and gravel into the air. I didn't know much how much more the boy could take, his pained screech cutting into my ears. I'd been hit like that before, and I didn't get back up.

I hurried around Charlotte and slid to a stop before the pipes.

I could see almost immediately what Driscoll had done. He

hadn't damaged the ward so much as taken its power source away. The compartment that held the vessel was cracked open and was nowhere to be found. "Fire the gun and throw it to me!"

Charlotte didn't hesitate. She took a shot at Cathal as he raised a sword to bring an end to Theodore, who now lay on the ground, struggling to breathe through his broken ribs. The aether gun fired, and a hole appeared in Cathal's torso. The faerie stumbled backward and collapsed against the inn. It wasn't an instant kill. He was still a threat.

Betsy's sword clanged against Driscoll's, and her words reverberated through my mind. *Fix the ward.*

Charlotte hurled the aether gun at me. I caught it and popped the cylinder out of the side, fumbling to get the vessel out of it as quickly as possible. It felt as though the motion took forever, as Driscoll landed a blow against Betsy and sent her tumbling to the ground beside Theodore. Charlotte pulled the throwing knife out of her vambrace and hurled it at Driscoll.

The thump of blade on flesh was sickening. The lack of expression on Driscoll's face was terrifying.

I finally slid the vessel out of the cylinder and slammed it home in the ward. The plate glowed, and for a moment, my breath left me as a force I didn't fully understand burst through the area.

Driscoll stumbled backwards. He reached out, as if he couldn't see what was in front of him. With the trinity in place, the world was snatched from the Unseelie fae. At least for a time.

Charlotte charged. Betsy held the sword up to her, and Charlotte grabbed it near the hilt. It was a dangerous move, it would cut deep into her palm, but the shortened blade made her strike faster than it would otherwise be. It slid cleanly up through Driscoll's jaw, only stopping when it hit the top of his skull. Charlotte screamed as she bowled into him.

Cathal struggled to his feet, shouting, "Where are you! What have you done!"

The harmonica pistol boomed once, twice, and as the warded projectiles passed through the wall that the aether had created, they turned into something more akin to a flaming cannonball. There were few creatures that could survive an eight-inch hole torn through their chest. There were fewer still that could survive two. I fired two more into Cathal, until his body caught fire and he collapsed on the ground.

I looked over to Charlotte, to my wife, as she wrapped her hand in a length of cloth torn from Driscoll's shirt. I stared at Driscoll for a time, the dagger-like blade gleaming in the cavern of his mouth, embedded in the skull.

"Theodore," Betsy said. "Stay awake. Are you okay?"

"Oh yeah," Theodore said. "Our plan went so smoothly, I hardly got a scratch. Except for all these broken ribs."

He started to laugh, and the sound changed to a groan of pain.

"Is he coughing up blood?" I asked.

"Not that I can tell," Betsy said.

"Good. He'll be fine."

"What about them?" Theodore asked.

"We bury them," I said. "Bury them under the conservatory. With this." I held up the aether gun.

"Are you sure?" Charlotte asked. "That was awfully effective."

"It's too dangerous. We won't need it now that the wards are active."

"You could destroy it," Betsy said. "But I wouldn't. You might have friends that are fae, but you also have enemies of all sorts."

I glanced at Charlotte and met her eyes.

She smiled and said, "Don't we always."

EPILOGUE

*S*urprised to find the front door locked, I tucked the wooden crate I was carrying under my arm so I could reach the keys in my leather vest. It had been three months since our encounter with Driscoll, and while I wouldn't say things had returned to normal, exactly, they had certainly calmed down. But Charlotte and I had both taken to locking the doors more than we used to.

The repairs on the conservatory were completed without much trouble, and what trouble there was Theodore had handled with a brilliant bit of brass work. We'd needed the payment, and Mihail hadn't let us down.

Perhaps most surprising, Roman Bishop had kept his word. Our slightly strange whiskey was now a staple at the local bar, and Bishop was confident he could find more buyers than I could make moonshine for. It was a challenge I was ready to take on.

The door swung open, and I blinked at the feet on the ladder beside my head.

"I was going to fix that this weekend," I said, carefully edging my way into the shop where the gentle tones of a repaired chime greeted me.

"Of course you were," Charlotte said, brushing off her hands as she climbed down from the ladder. She slapped a small tool belt against my chest, and I fumbled to catch it.

"Sounds great." I moved to set the tools onto the workbench before setting the crate beside them. "Mihail said the amulets worked great."

"How did he test them?" Charlotte asked, sitting down behind her workbench.

I shrugged. "Don't know. Don't know if I want to know."

Charlotte leaned forward as I took a crowbar to the wooden crate.

"Are those the bottles?" she asked.

I nodded, levered the length of metal, and pried the top off the crate with a squeal and a pop. The individual bottles weren't so heavy as I pulled one out, and I suspected the crate itself had made up a good deal of the weight.

Charlotte stood up and joined me, sliding her own bottle of smoked glass out and running her finger across the golden lettering etched into the side. She read the words aloud: "Warded Whiskey, The Tinkers' Drink."

I shook my head. "Nice craftsmanship on the bottles. Not a huge fan of the name."

Charlotte blew out a puff of air. "It already paid off a quarter of our debt. Bishop can call it whatever the hell he wants if that keeps up."

"Why don't we have Theodore and Betsy over tonight to celebrate?" I said with a smile.

"Okay," Charlotte said. "Just make sure they come through the front door."

I glanced back at the chimes Charlotte had fixed, and laughed.

We hope you enjoyed this story in the Legends of Havenwood Falls series featuring a variety of supernatural creatures. The series is a collaborative effort by multiple authors.

Books in the historical Legends of Havenwood Falls series:

Lost in Time by Tish Thawer
Dawn of the Witch Hunters by Morgan Wylie
Redemption's End by Eric R. Asher
Trapped Within a Wish by Brynn Myers
Blood and Damnation by Belinda Boring (August 2018)
Fated Beginnings by E.J. Fechenda (September 2018)

More books releasing on a monthly basis

Also try the signature NA/Adult series, Havenwood Falls, and the YA series, Havenwood Falls High

Stay up to date at www.HavenwoodFalls.com

Subscribe to our reader group and receive free stories and more!

ABOUT THE AUTHOR

Eric is a former bookseller, cellist, and comic seller currently living in Saint Louis, Missouri. A lifelong enthusiast of books, music, toys, and games, he discovered a love for the written word after being dragged to the library by his parents at a young age. When he is not writing, you can usually find him reading, gaming, or buried beneath a small avalanche of Transformers. Find him at http://www.ericrasher.com/.

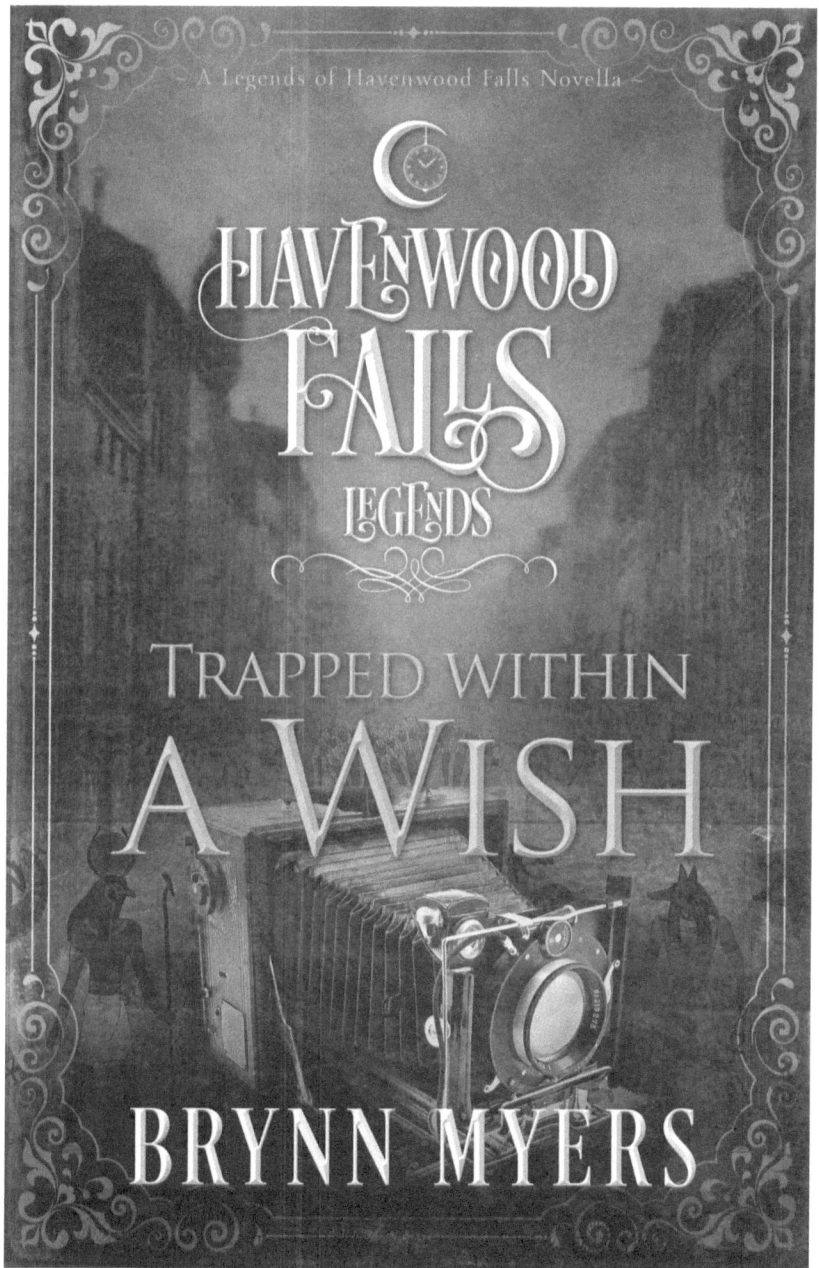

A Legends of Havenwood Falls Novella

HAVENWOOD FALLS LEGENDS

TRAPPED WITHIN A WISH

BRYNN MYERS

AN EXCERPT

Trapped Within a Wish (A Legends of Havenwood Falls Novella) by Brynn Myers

For eighteen years, Nathan Wade has searched for answers regarding his father's disappearance. Now, in 1920, he receives a letter from Calla Lily Mircea saying she's in possession of some of his father's belongings in a town called Havenwood Falls. Nathan wonders how a field camera lost on an archeological dig in Egypt could end up in a small town in Colorado, but something draws him in. Nathan takes the leap of faith, only to have his world turned upside down when he finds not only the camera, but a hidden treasure within.

Amani lost everything the day she came of age and her true nature was revealed. Now, having been trapped for eighteen years, her only hope is that someone will save her from the hell she's had to endure. When a handsome stranger inadvertently releases her, the wait is over, and the truth of her imprisonment comes to light.

Nathan and Amani are now bound to one another and determined to piece together the past. Someone wanted her gone, and she and Nathan race to solve the mystery that connects them both before it's too late.

TRAPPED WITHIN A WISH

AN EXCERPT

The hallway of New York University bustled with students roaming around—some were on their way to exams, while others were chatting about the upcoming summer break.

In his office on campus, Nathan Wade rifled through term papers, trying to find a student's dissertation on the 42 Laws of Ma'at when the door to his office opened, startling him.

"Is this what you've been waiting for?" Lillian asked as she entered the room.

"I don't know, Ms. Hartman. What is it?" Nathan replied as he continued to shuffle through the stack of papers in his hands.

"Enough with that formal business, young man. There are no students around," Lillian scoffed as she wagged the paper she held in the air. "This came in about an hour and a half ago, but you were teaching, and I didn't think it was important enough to interrupt the class to give it to you," she replied with a sly grin. "And why is he sending telegraphs anyway? Has he forgotten we're in the twentieth century? It is 1920, after all."

Nathan shook his head and chuckled under his breath. "What did Edgar have to say with his antiquated form of communication?"

Lillian reached for the silver chain holding her cheaters and pulled them on to see the words clearer. She read the two words and clicked her tongue in frustration. "Nothing yet."

"Nothing yet, what?"

"That's it. That's all it says." Lillian walked over to her desk and sat down. "I do not know why you continue to pay him to look for your father's satchel—it and the camera are long gone." She shook her head slowly. "I'm sorry. I know that is not what you want to hear, but it's true. It's been eighteen years, son. You have to move past this." Her tone shifted from judgmental to soft as she took off her glasses and let them hang around her neck.

"I can't stop searching and you know why," Nathan said as he stared into the eyes of the woman who'd cared for him after his father's disappearance.

Lillian Hartman was widowed, like his father had been. Before Nathan was born, Lillian and her husband, Charles, had been neighbors and close friends with his parents. When Nathan's mother died of consumption, Lillian became Nathan's surrogate mother. Then, after his father disappeared, she and Charles raised Nathan—gave him a life in lieu of his loss.

When Charles passed away a few years ago, Lillian was in need of a hobby to keep her mind busy. All that unused energy was going to waste, and Nathan was in need of an office assistant, now that he was an associate professor at the university. Lillian was the perfect assistant and the most qualified candidate to manage all of Nathan's pastimes.

"Nathan," Lillian soothed, "the clue to where your father disappeared to is not in that camera. Edgar can search the world over and still conclude what we already know. Sam and the camera are gone."

"I want to know what happened, Lillian. Not knowing is what binds me to this quest."

"But some mysteries will never be unraveled. You simply have to move on."

Nathan bowed his head and whispered, "I know."

"You're better suited spending your energy uncovering the mysteries found in those Egyptian tombs you love so much." She grinned and then threw her hands in the air. "That reminds me. I received notification from Howard Carter's office about an expedition opportunity. I'm not certain how that will work with your current class schedule, though."

Nathan glanced up. "They requested me?"

"Yes," she said, handing him the letter. "Here, read it. It's very complimentary."

"Wow, I didn't expect that," Nathan said as he put on his glasses to read the letter. When he read the last line, he grinned appreciatively. "It is indeed very complimentary, but sadly, I'm going to have to pass on this offer and use my time here to study linguistics in my off time." He sighed. "Maybe they'll ask again, for another dig. I can't imagine there won't be more to come."

"Always wanting to learn more. You always were such a curious boy."

"I received word that new funerary texts have arrived at the Metropolitan Museum of Art. They'll need to be translated, and as you have pointed out, it may do me some good to dive into a distraction."

Lillian picked up a stack of mail from the inbox on the corner of her desk and started to flip through it. As she did, she pulled her glasses back on and examined one envelope with an odd symbol pressed into a wax seal.

"Who uses letter seals anymore?" she mumbled under her breath. "Well, I guess whoever this is from," Lillian said to herself as she reached for her letter opener.

Lillian pulled out the neatly folded letter and read the words, disbelief and shock contorting her face with each word she read.

Dear Mr. Wade,

I'm writing this letter to inform you I am in possession of a camera I believe belongs to you. Inside the top flap of the tattered brown leather case is a tag with this New York address. The inscription reads, Samuel N. Wade. I do hope I've not contacted the wrong person in error and that this field camera indeed belongs to you. When you receive this, please reply to the address listed on the envelope.

Sincerely,

Calla Lily Mircea

"What's wrong, Lillian?" Nathan asked.

"Someone in," she paused to flip over the envelope, "Havenwood Falls has found your father's camera. They even have the bag," Lillian muttered. "I can't believe it."

"Where is Havenwood Falls?"

"According to the postage mark, it's someplace in Colorado."

"Colorado?" Nathan exclaimed. "How in the hell did the camera get there? It has to be a mistake. Egypt to some random place in the middle of nowhere is a bit of a stretch, don't you think?"

Lillian nodded, still trying to comprehend the words she'd just read. Sam's camera had been missing for as long as he had been, and no one, besides Nathan, thought they'd ever see it again. She eyed him over her glasses. "Nathan, I don't want you to get your hopes up."

Nathan took the letter from Lillian and stared at the words on the page for a moment before responding. "It may be nothing, but this is the first lead we've had. I will have to contact this Calla Lily and find out for myself."

"No, you can send Edgar. That is why you hired him, is it not?"

Nathan sighed. "It is, but there is something odd about this letter—this woman's writing. I feel like this is it. This," Nathan paused, "this is my father's camera, Lillian. I have to do this."

"Oh, Nathan," she replied gently.

"Look, it won't hurt anyone. Only another week and classes will be out for summer break. I can go then, and that way nothing will be affected here."

Lillian laid her hand on Nathan's. "This could indeed be a mistake, but I understand what you're saying. I will cover you here. I want you to have peace of mind, and I need you to find closure and put your father's death behind you."

"What if it is his? What if he is alive and has been living in Colorado all this time?"

She pulled him into a hug. "Then I guess that is all the more reason for you to go," she said as she stepped back. "Either way, you'll have an answer."

Nathan nodded. "I don't know, Lillian. I have a feeling I can't shake."

"Well, then let me respond to this Miss Mircea and make the arrangements for you to stay a few days," she said, before she kissed him on the forehead and walked over to her desk.

"This had better not be another dead end," Nathan mumbled under his breath as the gentle clicks of the typewriter sounded in the background.

The week passed by quickly, and Nathan was almost ready to go. Lillian had made all the arrangements with Calla Lily for Nathan to stay at Whisper Falls Inn upon his arrival. She also made sure Nathan's colleagues were aware he'd only be gone a short period of time on a fact-finding mission and would be back before summer's end at the latest.

Lillian thought back to when Samuel disappeared. He'd been working at the excavation site for Hatshepsut's tomb in the Valley of the Kings. Everything was going as expected according to his correspondence, and then one day they received a telegraph stating he'd gone missing—simply vanished, no trace of him found by the other Egyptologists on the dig. The only evidence they had was from a worker who reported seeing him taking a photograph of two young women near the excavation site.

Nathan had convinced himself that his father's satchel was the key to finding out what happened. He'd go on and on about photos, or maybe something Samuel found, and how it could show not only inside information about the tomb, but could also provide clues as to what happened on that day. Either way, Lillian worried about how all of this would affect Nathan in the end. Not knowing left him sad, but hungry for information—a conclusion could leave him broken.

Lillian hoped this trip to Havenwood Falls would confirm the final piece of the puzzle and finally let Nathan accept the truth—Sam met with foul play that fateful day, and the camera and any other belongings were long gone from this world. She typed up the last page for the itinerary and slipped it out of the typewriter wheel with a zing, placing it neatly on her desk. As soon as Nathan returned from afternoon class, she'd let him know the whos, whats, and whens for his departure tomorrow.

The door opened with a click and startled Lillian.

"Finished," Nathan called out as he entered the office. "The only thing left to do is mark the grades and submit them, then it's off to Colorado."

"I've made the final arrangements," she said as she stood. "You'll be taking the train into Montrose, Colorado, and Miss Mircea will meet you there. Apparently, they don't have direct access other than a bus to take you into the town itself, so she's offered to be your means of transportation."

Nathan gave her an odd look.

"Yes, my thoughts exactly, but considering your insistence that you yourself flesh this one out, you will have to abide by the rules set forth by the woman who has the satchel," Lillian said with a slight grin.

"Then I shall take it all at face value," Nathan replied, returning her smile. "Did she say where to meet her?"

"No, only that she'd be there when the train arrived, and she'd be on a bench near the platform."

"Okay then," he sighed.

"Have you finished packing?" Lillian asked as she began to sort the papers Nathan had set on her desk.

"Oh you know, I still have a few things to pack," he replied shyly.

"Nathan Allan Wade. I swear, will you never change?" Lillian laughed out loud. "Go home and get packed this instant."

Nathan grinned, knowing his truth was revealed. He hadn't packed a thing, but he was only going to be gone a few days. Nathan didn't see the point in bringing his dress attire. Instead, he'd settle for his field clothes: a couple of sport shirts, casual trousers, and a pair of suspenders.

"I don't have that much . . ." He relented under Lillian's motherly gaze.

"Nonetheless, off you go," Lillian said, shooing him out the door. "And don't forget to stop by the bank on the way home. You should have plenty of cash with you—enough to last the week at least."

"How about dinner tonight at six at Lombardi's?" Nathan asked as he grabbed his coat and hat.

"That sounds lovely, but only if you've done as I've asked and will be ready to leave in the morning. Your train departs at seven, and you cannot be late," Lillian chided.

"I will not only be ready to leave but will have my bags by the door." Nathan grinned. "I'll pick you up at five thirty," he said as he opened the door to leave.

"Five thirty it is." Lillian waved him out.

Nathan stopped by the bank, as Lillian suggested, and then the library. He needed to grab a book or two to keep his mind occupied on the train. It was, after all, going to take a few days to get to Colorado.

It was five thirty sharp when Nathan knocked on the door of Lillian's apartment. She was always a stickler for being on time, and Nathan knew if he was late, she'd balk over needing to rush to dinner. He adored Lillian and wanted nothing more than to make her happy. They lived in separate apartments, but within the same building. Lillian lived on the floor below his, and as they headed down the stairs, Nathan remembered carrying his father's satchel clumsily down each flight before his dad left for his latest expedition. He'd set it down on the last step and taken Lillian's hand as Samuel told her when he'd be returning. That was the last time he saw his father. It was also the day Lillian became his guardian.

"I want you to order whatever you like tonight, and no scrimping because you're worried about the cost, understand?" Nathan insisted.

"Oh no, you will not," Lillian scolded. "We're going to have a lovely dinner, but it will be on me." Nathan started to protest but stopped when she gave him "the look." "Besides, if you pay, I will assume it is to say goodbye, and I will not be saying goodbye to you, young man. You'll return in a week, and when you do, you can buy dinner then." She winked.

"Deal," Nathan replied as he raised his arm in the air to hail a cab.

"We can walk, Nathan."

"I didn't want you to have to walk all that way," he replied as the car pulled up to the curb. "And you gave no stipulation about a taxi, only dinner."

Nathan opened the door and offered his hand to her.

Lillian clicked her tongue, but didn't argue. Instead, the two rode to the restaurant, enjoyed a lovely meal, and returned home early enough for her to be able to read a chapter in her book before heading to bed. Nathan had left before on excursions, but he always came home. Something about him leaving this time felt different, though. They hugged one another tightly as they said their goodbyes.

"Don't worry. I'll be home in a week," Nathan insisted as he kissed her forehead. "I love you, Lillian."

"I love you too, Nathan. Now be careful. I'll hold the fort down here until you return."

He smiled. "You always do."

Nathan looked back one last time before he headed upstairs.

Purchase *Trapped Within a Wish* by Brynn Myers at your favorite book retailer.

www.ingramcontent.com/pod-product-compliance
Lightning Source LLC
Chambersburg PA
CBHW052010170626
46808CB00007B/2868